STRAIGHT BEAST MODE

Lock Down Publications & Ca$h Presents
STRAIGHT BEAST MODE
A Novel by *De'Kari*

Lock Down Publications

P.O. Box 944
Stockbridge, Ga 30281

Visit our website at www.lockdownpublications.com

Book interior design by: **Shawn Walker**
Edited by: **Tamira Butler**

Stay Connected with Us!

Text **LOCKDOWN** to 22828 to stay up-to-date with new releases, sneak peaks, contests and more…
Or **CLICK HERE** to sign up.

Thank you.

Submission Guideline

Submit the first three chapters of your completed manuscript to ldpsubmissions@gmail.com, subject line: Your book's title. The manuscript must be in a .doc file and sent as an attachment. Document should be in Times New Roman, double spaced and in size 12 font. Also, provide your synopsis and full contact information. If sending multiple submissions, they must each be in a separate email.

Have a story but no way to send it electronically? You can still submit to LDP/Ca$h Presents. Send in the first three chapters, written or typed, of your completed manuscript to:

LDP: Submissions Dept
P.O. Box 944
Stockbridge, Ga 30281

*DO NOT send original manuscript. Must be a duplicate. *

Provide your synopsis and a cover letter containing your full contact information.

Thanks for considering LDP and Ca$h Presents.

Chapter 1

Forest Hill

"Everybody get the fuck on the ground, now! You mutha-fuckas know what time it is. If I gotta repeat myself, then muthafuckas are gonna start dying in dis bitch! Move! Move! Move!" The deep rough baritone voice giving the command sounded somewhere in between a lion roaring and the sound of thunder.

The voice was alarming, yet it didn't match the 5'7", 185-pound frame that it came from. If Don's size wasn't intimidating, the all-black AR-15 with an extended 50 clip and sound suppressor on it was scary as fuck!

Sterling Bank Trust located at 115 West Portal Avenue was fairly empty, considering it was forty-five minutes until the lunchtime rush. There were only eleven people inside the bank. All eleven inside the bank immediately stopped what they were doing once they laid eyes on the three masked gunmen with extremely big guns who just stormed the bank.

"Keep yo' muthafuck'n hands up in front of your head like Superman! Act like you muthafuckas are flying! I swear to God, if yo' hands do anything except act like you're flying, I'mma fill you with some hot shit!" Don continued to order as he swept both his eyes and the assault rifle in his hands over everybody that was on the ground.

XO didn't waste any time running past his cousin, Don. He knew exactly where he was going, who he was looking for, and what he was supposed to do. More importantly, he knew exactly how much time he had to do it. His blood was rushing through his veins like raging rapids as his adrenaline soared from his excitement. XO was a real street nigga who lived for action. At 30 years old, he'd been in the streets for over ten years. He had enough money that he could fall back from the streets and from living a life of crime. He still was waist deep in the shit simply because he loved the thrill.

XO ran over to the cubicle that Mary Anne Moore sat at and snatched the middle-aged white woman off the ground by her dyed auburn hair. She cried out in pain and sheer fear. Once she was standing on her feet face to face with him, XO looked directly into her emerald-green eyes and spoke calm and clear.

"Mary, I am only going to tell you this once, so listen closely. Right now, both Jessica and Lil' Anthony are tied up along with your babysitter, Jackie Hill, in your lovely two-story house on Lincoln Blvd." He showed her the screen of the phone he was holding in his free hand.

Mary Anne was terrified. Yet, the mention of her 10 and 12-year-old children gave her alarm enough to look at the screen. Instantly, she grabbed her heart as if she was having a heart attack. She was seeing a live Facetime feed of her children and babysitter all tied up and laying on the floor in the living room. Tears instantly formed in her eyes. XO knew he had Mary Anne right where he wanted her. "If you don't do exactly what I tell you, when I tell you, my nigga is gonna make sure you start making funeral arrangements. Do you understand what I'm saying to you, bitch?" His eyes were jet-black pools of evil as she looked at them through the openings in the ski mask.

"Y-yes, I-I-I'll do whatever you say, j-just please don't hurt my children. Please!" She could feel the evil energy coming off the man standing before her and knew he wouldn't hesitate to do as he said he would do.

"Let's go!" He snatched her by her red Donna Karan cardigan sweater and pushed her forcefully toward the cage that led to the safe.

"Two minutes thirty seconds!" Murda called out like a football coach. His eyes kept a constant back-and-forth rhythm from the sniveling muthafuckas on the floor to the scene outside the bank and to his watch.

Murda was XO's 27-year-old little brother. At 5'10" and 230 pounds, he looked like a human bulldog. However, it wasn't his size that earned him the name Murda. It was the ease with which he could kill and the nonchalant way he went on about his business after he killed somebody. He literally acted like nothing happened.

Don's eyes were like precision binoculars as they scanned the room, paying attention to every single detail, waiting for someone to step out of line. He hoped none of these white folks would test his gangsta. They would easily find out it wasn't a game, if they did.

"Why do you people always have to cause problems and take what isn't yours? Why don't you get a fucking job?" Neither Don nor Murda could believe what they had just heard!

It was Don who reacted. "What'd you just say, bitch?" he growled at the short, brown-head, mousy-looking woman who called out.

"You people are always doing something to us poor good folk with your gangster wannabe music and your drugs and—" Before she could get another word out, Don kicked her as hard as he could in her racist, shit-talking mouth. The woman's smartass words were replaced with a fountain of blood and broken teeth. He didn't stop there. Don proceeded to stomp the dumb bitch like Kane did that bald head nigga in *Menace to Society*.

"Stupid bitch, I bet you next time you shut the fuckup while gangstas are handling business," he told her unconscious body as he continued to stomp her head into the ground, ignoring the pool of blood that began to form under her head.

The rest of the hostages that witnessed the display of utter lack of human life cringed from the gruesome sight before their eyes. Even though the woman's skull was cracked, Don didn't stop punishing her until Murda called out.

"Blood, that's enough! Fuck that bitch and get back on point!"

Don stopped stomping the woman and gave a menacing look at his younger cousin. Don didn't like anybody telling him what to do. The only two things stopping him from getting in Murda's ass or saying something slick, was Murda's quick temper and the fact that he was right. By focusing on the bitch he was stomping, he wasn't aware of what everyone else was doing. Which meant he wasn't doing what he was supposed to be doing. Still being defiant, he kicked the stupid, slick-talking bitch in the face one more time before getting back on point.

XO was moving as fast as his two arms would allow him to go. Already, he had one full duffel bag on the floor next to his feet. He was in the process of filling up the second one. Mary Anne sat cowered down at the end of the metal counting table that was inside the huge vault.

"One minute five seconds!" he heard Murda call out from the front of the bank.

Out of the corner of his eye, XO saw Mary Anne reaching for something. When he turned his head toward her to get a better look to see what she was doing, he noticed the button on the side of the table for the first time. The button was no doubt some sort of alarm, he figured. He was too far away from her to get to her in time to stop her from pressing the button.

Without thinking, he dropped the stacks of money that were in his hand and upped the AR-15 that was strapped in front of his chest and pulled the trigger. A split second later, a cloud of pinkish red flew out the other side of Mary Anne's head, as the three bullets spit out of the silenced barrel and crashed into her head, knocking a patch out of her shit. Her body spasmed violently after it hit the floor.

XO still had forty-five seconds left to keep filling up the bag. *Fuck that!* he thought to himself. A murder that was committed during a robbery was a capital offense. XO wasn't

10

trynna to see that. If XO was going out, it would be like a true gangsta. In a blaze of glory. He swiftly snatched up the last three bundles that were in front of him and tossed them into the duffel bag.

He snatched the full duffel bag off the floor and threw it over his shoulder, then he snatched the second bag off the table. He gave one final look at Mary Anne's body that had stop moving now that she was dead. *Mary Anne will never know that XO just spared her the tragedy of going home, only to find the dead bodies of her children and their babysitter.* Then he got the fuck out of the vault.

The moment Murda saw his brother come barging out of the vault, he knew something was wrong. Murda looked at his watch to see if he was mistaken. Just as he'd figured, it was still thirty-four seconds left for XO to grab money. If he was coming out early, something was wrong. Murda raised his Mach-90 and turn toward the front door, ready to make sure they made it out without any problems.

XO handed the second duffel bag to Don, who threw it over his shoulder. Once the bag was secure, Don followed Murda out of the front door. XO walked backward behind him, making sure there was no one being a superhero. When he was sure that no one was going to do anything stupid, he turned around and ran out of the front door as well.

Pedestrians screamed and ran for cover at the sight of the masked gunmen running out of the bank. Later, the only things anyone would be able to recall was the fact that all of the men carried what looked like machine guns. And they all got into a dark-colored SUV that was parked outside of the bank. Dell (the getaway driver) sped off after XO jumped into the back of the stolen Jeep Grand Cherokee SRT. He sped down West Portal until he jumped on Highway 1, which was less than a quarter mile down the road. They rode Highway 1 South until they reached the Lake Shore exit. Dell headed east on Ocean Avenue until they reached Mount Davidson Manor, where they had two clean vehicles parked and waiting for them. Dell and Don jumped inside of the Chevy Impala while the two brothers jump inside of XO's souped-up Grand National. All four men drove off, each car taking separate routes back to Double Rock.

"Why'd you come out of the bank early?" Murda asked his big brother as he drove.

"A nigga was filling up the second duffel when that stupid ass bitch forced a nigga to knock her block off. Bitch was trying to hit the alarm on the kid like I wasn't on my shit. After I pushed her shit back, wasn't no question, it was time to get the fuck out of there," XO told him as he was driving on Highway 280 East.

Murda hated the thought of bust'n a move and leaving money behind. He knew his brother was right and made the best decision, but it still didn't make him feel any better. It felt like they were taking a loss, and Murda didn't take losses. He knew there wasn't any sense crying over spilled milk either. Therefore, he said "fuck it!" mentally. At least they made it out of that bitch together.

Chapter 2

"Run up in the bank bitch, hit the deck/Yo bust money, and get the keys off his neck (come here)/We on the clock, three minutes until we finished/Feds are on the way, but I'm tryin' to see spinach/In and out, duffel bag across the back/Extra-long sports coat to cover up the mack/Feds they attack, I spit lead out niggas spread out/Run up on a civilian in his car, make him get out."

DMX's raspy voice rapped "Heat" loudly out of the speakers at the Clubhouse. The Clubhouse was a three-bedroom house located on C-Block, right in the heart of Double Rock. It was the hangout and heart of the 357 Mobb, the most ruthless gang to ever come out of Double Rock. Not even the infamous and respected TMB, or Touch Money Boys, were fucking with the 357 Mobb. Whereas TMB was getting their money, the 357 Mobb was getting their body count up. On top of that, they were getting to the money, chasing money like a Billy Goat.

The entire front of the house looked like a music video shoot. The weed smoke was strong enough and thick enough for a nigga to smoke the air and get high off the contact. Piles and piles of money were all over the living room and dining room tables next to multiple money counters. Also, on the tables were ashtrays filled with blunts as well as blunt roaches, along with various types of liquor.

XO sat at the dining room table across from Don with a baby AR-15 sitting on his lap. On the right side of the money counter that he was using, there was a 9mm with an extended fifty clip sticking out of it. His brown skin, Lord Jesus dreadlocks, and Bin Laden beard made him resemble Damian Marley. The thirty-year-old killer was a walking definition of a shotta. His dreads were hanging over his face as his attention was on the pile of money in front of him that he was counting.

After he finished wrapping a rubber band around another $10,000 stack, Don looked across the table at his big cousin with a smirk on his face. He reached for his bottle of Hennessy and took a nice swig of it. Although Don and XO were cousins, their relationship was brotherly. Don could relate to XO more than he could relate to his three actual brothers. XO was a street nigga through and through. Like Murda, he had a quick temper and preferred to let his gun discuss any and all bullshit. XO wasn't doing no arguing with nobody. Don was a full-fledged animal who lived for the bullshit.

"Aye, turn that muthafuck'n shit off and check it out!" C1ty, the undisputed leader and boss of the 357 Mobb, walked into the living room from out of the master bedroom. No one stopped what they were doing or moved a muscle. In fact, there was no inclination whatsoever that anyone heard the command that was given.

"Oh, so a nigga in here talking to himself or something?" C1ty addressed everyone present. He turned his head, eyeing each person individually, his long dreadlocks resembling a lion's mane.

"Shit, you up in here barking orders like niggaz your bitches or something. On that East Coast shit. I think you've been reading too many of them urban books. Got you talking like John Gotti and shit. You might be the head of this shit, but nigga, respect, we all gangsters. Ain't no bitch up in here, cuz!" Murda didn't take his eyes off of what he was doing as he spoke.

"I know niggaz ain't up in dis bitch working with no muthafuck'n emotions. Talk'n 'bout we gangstas." C1ty raised both his hands and made quotations when he said "we gangstas."

Murda finished wrapping the rubber band around the $10,000 stack in his hand. He dropped the stack on the table when he was done and lifted his head to look at his little cousin.

"Never that. A nigga just stating facts. Facts that you going to have to respect," he told C1ty, staring directly into his eyes.

Everybody stopped what they were doing and were on full alert. The only sound in the house while the two cousins stared at each other was DMX's voice coming through the speakers. The tension in the room was thick.

"Respect it or what? Murda, nigga, is you threatening me?" C1ty's hand automatically went to his waist where he kept his .357 in case Murda started tripping.

"Come on, cousin, you of all people know I don't make threats. It is what it is, and I said exactly what I meant. But my nigga if you want some smoke, then that's cool too." Murda scooted his chair back and let his hand drop to the .44 Desert Eagle that was resting on his lap.

"Check this shit out, my nigga. We ain't about to have this shit today," CJ called out as he slowly stood from the couch and made his way over to the coffee table to pick the phone up that controlled the music to turn it down. "Murda, ain't nobody want no smoke up in dis bitch, so fall the fuck back and take your hand off that cannon. C1ty, on the real tho', my nigga Murda telling you some real shit. Sometimes you got the tendency to talk to niggaz like we some real bitches. You need to fall back on that shit, fo'real, my nigga. Now da music is down, tell us what's good." Before taking his seat, CJ looked over at Murda to ensure his hand was indeed off the gun.

CJ was usually the voice of reason when it came to the 357 Mobb. He was usually calm and quiet, except for when he was on his bi-polar shit. Then it was like Dr. Jekyll and Mr. Hyde. Calm, quiet CJ could turn into the Undertaker himself. He was also second in command of the team, which meant his word carried weight among them all.

Murda still had a cold look on his face, but he took his hand away from his gun. "My nigga, speak on it."

C1ty looked at Murda for a couple more seconds before he realized that CJ was right. Maybe he was a little militant or aggressive sometimes, but that's just how he was. That said, he could tell that sooner or later Murda was going to force his hand. He'd hate to have to knock a branch off of his own family tree. But like Murda said, "it is what it is." He brought his mind back to business.

"That shit's on every local channel right now, live as we speak." He looked over at XO, who was stroking his thick beard while paying attention. "XO, I already knew if you smacked that bitch, then she gave you a good muthafuck'n reason. That don't mean shit to them feds, though. And we can bet they about to be all over this shit like they was with the Oklahoma bombing. Especially since a grey girl was killed by what the witnesses are saying was a group of black men. Which they confirmed by watching the video clip inside the vault. XO, when you bent down to grab the duffel bag, a couple of your dreads fell out of the ski mask." C1ty walked over to the coffee table, grabbed the remote, and turned the big screen TV that was on the wall to the Fox News Channel 2.

The video clip of XO inside the vault was playing, and on the bottom of the screen a ticker played, saying, "Warning, video may display graphic images not suitable for young children." On the screen, they all watched XO filling the second duffel bag. The first one was already full and sitting on the floor next to him. All the while, a scared Mary Anne was on the ground crying while holding her eyes. Then they saw Mary Anne begin reaching for the hidden alarm button on the far side of the table. By the time XO noticed what was going on and reacted, her hand was inches away from the button.

The next thing they saw was XO reacting with lightning speed and blowing Mary Anne's head off. They watched as he grabbed the last of the money next to him and bent down to grab the duffel bag. Sure enough, about four dreadlocks fell out of his ski mask.

"Fuck," XO mumbled under his breath.

"Nigga, they ain't saying nothing! The whole city got dreads," Dell, the oldest of the brothers, spoke up for the first time. "That is the whole city, except us smart niggaz that ain't trynna to get hit with mistaken identity."

"Nigga, I'm way too smooth to grow some nappy ass dreads on this here head, nigga," CJ stated, rubbing his taper cut with deep waves.

"Nigga do got a point. The whole fucking city do got dreads, so that ain't 'bout to be about shit. All that means is the local pigs about to be fucking with every nigga they see with dreads. XO, you might want to lay low for a minute." Murda took a hefty pull on the blunt he'd been smoking.

"Got that right. But I think we should all lay low for a minute and let this shit blow over. It ain't like we're over here hurting for bread or nothing. We going to push the Pacific Height thang back a couple of weeks from the original date, and in the meantime, keep our ear to the streets and make sure everything is copasetic before we run up in that bitch and take what's rightfully ours." C1ty pointed to the money that everyone was counting before he continued. "We gonna see what this little shit right here do. Y'all already know that we gonna holla at OG Then we gonna get our eat on, like we always do." Everybody in the room just nodded their heads.

One of the family's mottos was "what's understood ain't got to be said." They already knew the get down. So, there was no need discussing things. They had all been doing their thing, getting money the "ski mask" way for years. Everybody in Bayview Hunters Point new about them boyz from the Allison Griffin Projects known as Double Rock. The family of jackers was serious about their money and deadly with that trigger play.

It was young Demario a.k.a C1ty who was the strategic one out of them all, with a very calculated mind and a natural foresight to put things into perspective that most men couldn't.

17

The one who came up with the idea of all the men coming together and getting money with each other as one cohesive unit rather than to risk their lives getting money with other niggaz. He also decided they should step up from small-time robberies of liquor stores, which Dell and Don were doing, and robbing drug dealers like Murda and XO were doing, to actually robbing credit unions and banks.

At first, Dell and Don weren't feeling the idea of hitting banks, but C1ty explained to them that if caught, you got the same amount of time for robbing a liquor store as you did a bank. Not only that, but there was sometimes twenty-five times the amount of money in the bank than it was in a liquor store. The deciding factor was C1ty pointing out damn near every liquor store in the hood carried guns and sometimes bust back. Whereas no one inside a bank carried a gun, except sometimes the old ass security guard.

Murda and XO were a different story all together. They didn't give a fuck as long as they were getting money the ski mask way. They both had realized that it was a trend that was spreading thru the hood, that drug dealers were now calling the police and testifying on niggaz. So, to them, the opportunity couldn't have come at a better time.

CJ was C1ty's right-hand man, and Wes was the loyal little brother to C1ty. So, it was only natural that they would be down with whatever C1ty put together. At the time, C1ty was 19, and it was clear to God, niggaz, and everybody in between that he was going to be a legend one day like the Shrimp Boy. A little over a year after forming 357 Mobb, C1ty was proven to be even more than what everyone expected he would be. He was currently the head of 357 Mobb, but he was slowly rising through the ranks of San Francisco's underworld.

"CJ, don't forget we got business in a little while." He looked over at his cousin, who just finished lining up his eighth stack of ten thousand.

"It's good. I'll be ready to roll out when it's the time, bro, don't trip," CJ responded.

C1ty nodded his head to CJ then looked over at Wes, who was the only one not counting money. His job was to watch the many monitors connected to the cameras around the house and watch the activities on the block.

"Lil' Brah, are you fucking with us tonight?" he asked.

"You already know, brah, don't trip," West replied, never taking his eyes off the monitors.

"Say less then. Dell, let me know when we're ready for OG," C1ty told his oldest brother.

"I got you," Dell assured him.

"Aight," C1ty called out just as his cell phone began ringing.

He pulled the phone out of his pocket and looked to see who was calling him. G-Baby's face was on the screen. He turned his 6'0", 165-pound frame around and headed to the back room to take the call.

Chapter 3

One of the flyest niggaz in San Francisco was twenty-year-old DeAndre Jordan a.k.a Lil' Dooka. The middle of four brothers, Lil' Dooka had felt his entire young life that he constantly had to outdo any and everyone around just to prove himself. Which he found himself doing constantly. As he pulled up to the red light, Lil' Dooka took the opportunity to inspect the wet, 360-degree spiral ocean sitting on top of his freshly tapered head. His waves were just as silky smooth as his deep, dark-chocolate skin. Without a doubt, Lil' Dooka was a ladies magnet. He had a stable full of hot, exotic young females, yet his heart belonged to one woman.

He pulled off once the stop light turned green, but not before turning the volume up on Yatta's song, "Youngboy." Lil' Dooka sang along with Yatta and Iamsu as they laced the track. When his part came on, Lil' Dooka became animated.

"Young boi, I've been on da block trynna to get it/big bands on me and my watch cost a ticket."

Yatta had already been gone a couple of years now. Sent to California Prison System too young like most of the young African American men who were born and raised in what was known as Killa Cali.

As he pulled up to the front of San Francisco University, Lil' Dooka saw all kinds of bad ass hotties of every shade, race, and flavor one could imagine. Nevertheless, it was the 5'6" Latina rocking the all-red Better Living sweatsuit that held his attention. The way her 32-C, 25-31-inch frame filled out the sweats who had every nigga anywhere in the vicinity eye fucking her as well.

When Gabriela saw the 2017, gun-metal Mustang GT with the TIO license plate, she lit up. It stopped directly in front of her with the sun gleaming off the fresh new wax job. Lil' Dooka and Gabriela locked eyes just before he hopped out the ride and strolled cockily over to where she was standing. The music blasted loudly out of the driver's door that he left wide open, drawing everyone's attention. All the haters and fuck niggaz who were just gawking at Gabriela instantly began mean mugging the shit out of Lil' Dooka as he walked boldly up to Gabriela, wrapped his arms around her, and proceeded to tongue her down like they were on the set of a live porno shoot.

The mugs on suckas' faces disappeared quicker than they appeared once they saw the big ass bulge sticking out of Lil' Dooka's Better Living T-shirt. Lil' Dooka finally broke the kiss and opened the door for his sweetheart. When she climbed inside, he closed the door and strolled just as confidently back to the driver's side like no one else was there at all. To add insult to injury, the suckas couldn't help but to read the slogan on the back of the shirt. "DON'T LET THAT BOTHER YOU!" Feeling fucked up, they all let it bother them.

"Daaaamn, Papi, did you see the way all the niggaz was screw-facing you? I thought I was going to have to get Queen Latifah on them and *Set It Off*!" Gabriela joked after she turned the music down.

Lil' Dooka didn't play about people fucking with his music. His Gabriela was the only person who could get away with it, and it still pissed him off when she did it.

"Naw, I wasn't stuntin' suckas. I was too busy sending telepathic signals to that camel toe you got sticking out of them damn sweats. And you know your lil' ass ain't 'bout to set nothing off but me if you keep fucking with my radio," he responded.

"Boi, please. I wish you would think shit was sweet around here. Don't think 'cuz I'm letting you hit this that you can't get fucked up too. 1237, nigga, anybody can get it!" she told him, trying her best to sound gangsta.

"Yeah, okay, stupid." He laughed.

Lil' Dooka loved when Gabriela talked that shit. Even though she was square as fuck, Gabriela came from a family that was full-fledged with the shit. She always told Lil' Dooka she wanted more out of life, which was why she was going to college. Yet, Gabriela swore on the Catholic Bible that she would buss that thang for him at the drop of a heartbeat if he ever needed her too. She swore she would do anything for him. Lil' Dooka wasn't listening to that shit. He knew bitches nowadays would say anything to a nigga.

"I was bored earlier, so I stopped by the mall and snatched those new Retros you wanted. They in the back," he told her as they were getting ready to turn onto Ocean Boulevard.

"Oh, daddy! Thank you!" Gabriela got juiced. She'd seen the new Jordans in a magazine the other day and just had to have them to go with her new Kappa sweatsuit she had just gotten.

She spun in her seat to pick the bag up as Lil' Dooka reached for a half-smoked blunt that he had in the ashtray. Gabriela didn't waste any time pulling the sneakers out of the box they were in. Excitedly, she leaned over and gave Lil' Dooka a kiss on the cheek, before thanking him again. He loved seeing her happy, which was why the moment she told him about the shoes, he made a mental note to buy her a pair. Shit, they were so clean, he ended up copping him a pair of them joints too.

They pulled into the parking lot of the Mayflower. It was a nice, quiet hole-in-the-wall that served just about anything you could think of, from Chinese food to soul food and everything in between. The food was off the chain, and everybody in San Francisco knew about it. Gabriela couldn't get enough of the food. So, whenever he picked her up from school, they would stop by the Mayflower and grab a bite to eat.

When they walked inside of the small, cozy restaurant, both of their mouths began watering. The smell of many different aromas was breathtaking. They found their own seat toward the back of the restaurant. From this particular spot, Lil'

Dooka could see a full view of the restaurant as well as the outside parking lot, eyes always open for any type of threat.

The waitress appeared at the table almost instantly. Her name was Christine. She was a young, slim, dark African American with average features and an average body. However, once she smiled, her face lit up. She had a beautiful, inviting smile.

"Hey, Gabby, girl, I saw you guys come in from back there in the kitchen. Girl, you are killing that sweat suit. I swear you and God had to be on good terms for him to bless you with that body," she flirted before looking over at Dooka and saying to him, "Dooka, I don't know why you keep thinking it's sweet bringing her in here every day like my mouthpiece ain't on point. Keep it up and I'mma have to show you what time it is."

Dooka and Gabriela both started laughing. "Christine, the only thing you taking from me is my order. I don't care how strong of a piece it is. Ma, you could never be Lil' Dooka. I'm da boi, sis, dat nigga times two. They don't flock to me 'cause of my mouthpiece. They flock to me 'cuz they know."

"Christine, how many times I gotta tell you that I don't fuck around like that? I needs me a real nigga wit' a real dick. That synthetic shit ain't working for me," Gabriela told her when she stopped laughing.

"Girl, you playing. If I put this heater head on that little thick ass of yours, you'll forget what a dick is." Christina was as serious as a heart attack. Her head game was remarkable.

Christina attended the university with Gabriela. Though the two women hardly saw each other on campus, when they did, they usually took the time to say a few words to one another. Every time the couple came into the restaurant, Christine was there. Over time, the three of them had become friendly.

"Well, I tell you what. If ever I lose my mind or get too drunk, I'll come find you and put this thang in your face. Until then, respect my king and bring him his food," Gabriela told her.

"Yeah, I'll be waiting too. Now, what do you guys want to order?" Christina prepared to take their order.

They gave Christine their order and she walked away heading toward the kitchen to place it, while imagining what Gabby's little pussy would taste like to her.

"I can't take you nowhere," Dooka joked with Gabriela once Christina walked away.

"Whatever. That heifer ain't got nothing to do with me."

"Yeah, I know, let me find out that's really yo' nigga when y'all at school," he continued to tease Gabriela.

"Let you find out? Nigga, let me find out you in here all getting jealous over lil' daddy with the waitress skirt on," Gabriela fired back her own joke.

The two of them laughed and joked with each other until their food came. After eating lunch, Dooka drove Gabriela home. She stayed in South San Francisco a.k.a South City. Which was a completely new world compared to San Francisco. Before dropping her off, Dooka gave Gabriela $500 for spending money. Lil' Dooka wasn't balling nor was he anywhere close to it. He was doing his thang, though. Lil' Dooka was the pill man in the hood. So, he wasn't a broke nigga either. He had plans to make it out of the hood. But for now, he was embracing it.

Lil' Dooka was on his way back to the hood when his cell phone started ringing. "Speak on it, nigga," he answered after seeing Turk's name on the screen.

"Where you at, brother?" Turk asked as soon as he heard Lil' Dooka's voice.

"Just leaving your bitch's house, stupid, why?" Lil' Dooka talked shit like always.

"Nigga, when I call dat bitch she better tell me you left that dough on the nightstand," Turk shot back.

"Nigga, the only thing I left that bitch was some nutt on her chin. Now, what's up?"

"Nigga I need you to slide thru once you land. Take some of these Benjamins and Johnsons off my hands right quick," Turk told him, sounding like Chris Tucker.

"Alright, bet. Say less. I'mma slide in a minute," Lil' Dooka let him know.

"Fa'sho, bet." Turk hung up the phone.

Lil' Dooka turned his music up and relit the half of the blunt he put out before going inside of the Mayflower. Twenty minutes later, he was pulling up on Turk at the 4-Lot. The 4-Lot was a parking lot in the hood where they kicked it at and trapped sometimes.

When Lil' Dooka pulled up, Turk had a couple of young bitches in front of him. The hoes looked like ratchets to Lil' Dooka, so he paid their ass no mind.

"Nigga, I just got off the phone wit' my bitch. She say yo' ass ain't left that money on the nightstand like you was supposed to do. And she say since you left, her shit ain't stopped itching. Nigga, let me find out you done gave my bitch dem lil' itchy muthafuckas," Turk clowned the moment he peeped Lil' Dooka walking up to him.

"You sound stupid. That's why I didn't touch her little ratchet ass. Bitch kept scratching. I'm outside the apartment and shit talking about did I want her to make me some breakfast. Bitch needs to make an appointment!" Lil' Dooka clowned right back. That's how they were.

The two of them along with MoMo, 4-Boy, Reco, Waka, Bubz, BR, and T.G. all grew up from the dirt together. When you'd known niggaz your whole life, it wasn't no friendships. It was a brotherhood. Especially in the borders of the hood.

Lil' Dooka embraced Turk in a one-arm embrace. "What's good wit' it, brother?"

"Shit. Trynna figure out which one of these two bitches I'mma break off with a dose of dick." Turk looked at the girl that was on his left and licked his lips at her before doing the same to the second girl. Both of them looked at him and giggled.

"You know me, though, I might just say fuck it and get my Jack Tripper on, nigga, *Three's Company*."

Everybody laughed just before Lil' Dooka told Turk to check it out. The two of them walked to Lil' Dooka's Mustang to conduct their business away from the two bitches.

"Ooh, bitch! Lil' Dooka's black ass is so fucking fine," Marlene told Stacy after Turk and Lil' Dooka walked off.

Marlene was what they called a "Slim Goody." She was very petite but had just the right amount of curves that made her body desirable. She was 5 '6," 155 pounds, and mixed with black and white.

"I know, bitch. Little black muthafucka running around here like a little Hershey Kiss and shit. Make a bitch wanna suck all over his little snicker," Stacy commented.

She was the complete opposite of Marlene physically. The only thing the two shared in common was their fair skin. Stacy was barely 5'2" and weighed 160 pounds. With her pineapple skin and super thick body, she was often told she resembled Red Bone Noe from the magazine. Her 36 D's were nice and firm, and her ass was bigger than Pinky's, the porn star.

"Bitch, from what Lelani told Jazzel, ain't nothing little about that nigga's snicker," Marlene corrected her. We should see if he trynna fuck wit' it. Bitch, we can fa'sho do the group thang."

"Bitch, as good as your ass eat pussy, we don't need neither one of them niggaz! You'll have a bitch ready to marry yo' tongue," Stacy teased her while she grabbed a handful of Marlene's little ass.

"Bitch, you sound stupid! For one, what I look like marrying your broke ass? We'd be two broke hoes like them two white bitches on TV show *2 Broke Girls*, and secondly, I'm not trynna to choose some pussy over some dick. I need dick in my life, bitch!"

Stacy was offended because she really had a thing for Marlene, but she played it off. "Bitch, you know I'm just jawz'n. Besides, I'm not trynna do no group shit. Every bitch from The Four (pronounced Foe') know Lil' Dooka ain't paying for it, and my lights are about to get turned off. As soon as Turk smells this muthafucka, he gone break a bitch off!"

Both of them started laughing hard. It was true. Turk was a wild child. He didn't give a fuck about nothing but his niggaz and having fun. He had plenty of money and threw that shit around like a stripper on a pole. To Turk, the only purpose money served was the fun he could have with it.

"Fuck is you bitches laughing at?" Turk asked as he and Dooka came walking back up.

"It ain't 'bout shit. We was just wondering if Dooka was trynna fuck wit' us. You know, all of us having some fun." Marlene looked seductively in Lil' Dooka's eyes as she spoke. She could feel the moisture leaking from her pussy just from looking at Dooka.

"Yeah! Yeah! That's that shit right there! That shit a nigga talking about!" Turk was juiced. He could already picture watching his dick slide in and out of Stacy's thick, yellow ass. "What's up, brother, you gone fuck wit' us and help me show these bitches how niggaz from the 4 do it?"

Looking at the size of that ass that was on the back of Stacy made Lil' Dooka's dick rise. He would love to have her thick ass bouncing up and down on his shit. Plus, he already knew from niggaz in the hood that Marlene had that fire.

Stacy peeped the way Lil' Dooka was looking up and down her body. She stood back on her legs so her breasts would stand put and her ass would stand up. She knew without a doubt it was about to be on and popping. She figured she would seal the deal by asking, "Lil' Dooka, you think you can handle all this ass?" She emphasized by slapping herself on her ass cheeks. Her big ole booty shook like an earthquake.

"I'm not even 'bout to front, lil' momma. I'd probably have yo' lil' thick ass unable to walk for a couple of weeks. But I'mma have to catch y'all next time. I gotta bust some moves and get this paper." Lil' Dooka hated to turn down the offer, but pussy wasn't putting no money in his pockets. He'd let them other niggaz have fun. He would have his fun later.

"What! Come on, brotha. Nigga, da money gonna be there. Let's do our porn star thang. We can get the money later." Turk couldn't believe the shit that just came out of Lil' Dooka's mouth.

"That's where you got me fucked up, brother. The pussy gone always be there. Money is just like time; it waits for no man. I don't have enough of either one of them, time or money. Right now, I'mma get this money." Lil' Dooka turned around and started to walk away. After three or four steps, he looked over his shoulder at Stacy. "Next time, lil' mama, you can make it rain over a nigga all night." He winked at her.

"I'mma hold your fine ass to that too." Stacy was dead serious. She couldn't help but to bite her bottom lip, trying to be her sexiest.

"It's all good, boo, you do that," he told her before walking back to his car and pulling off.

Chapter 4

"Hello?" Dooka finally answered the phone on the third ring.

"What's up, fool? What took you so long to answer the phone, you getting some pussy or something?" The sound of Chino's voice was so loud. Lil' Dooka had to adjust the volume on his phone before he replied.

"Naaw, nigga, I'm on the toilet taking a shit," Lil' Dooka told him, hoping Chino didn't really want shit.

After leaving Turk and them two little ratchets, he came to his house to break down his last boat of Facebook E-pills. They were his best sellers. Them and the Instagrams. Both pills were triple stacks that hit like quadruples. Halfway through fucking with the pills, Lil' Dooka's stomach started doing somersaults like an Olympic Gymnastics Team. He'd been on the toilet for the past fifteen minutes with a severe bout of bubble guts.

"Well, wipe that shit and get ready, 'cause I need to holla at you!" Chino yelled into the phone.

"Chino, nigga, now ain't good. A nigga got them bubble guts. I'm not about to drive all the way the fuck to yo' hood and be shitting all on myself." Just then, another gut-wrenching stream shot out his ass, strong enough to hurt his stomach.

"It's good, fool, you ain't gotta go nowhere. I'm already on the way to you. So, get ready."

"Damn, Chino! Alright, nigga, bet, you better be talking some shit I'm trynna hear and not be talking that bullshit. Give me like fifteen minutes, bro, and I got you." Lil' Dooka felt like his entire stomach was about to drop out his ass.

"Can't do that, homie. I just pulled up out front. Wipe yo' black ass and open the door. And make sure you wash yo' hands too, fool," Chino told Lil' Dooka before disconnecting the call.

Lil' Dooka shook his head as he sat his phone on the bathroom sink and reached for the toilet paper. He liked Chino 'cause he was crazy as shit, like a real nigga. Chino was an up-and-coming Soldia for the 21st Hogg Status gang. 21st was the chapter of the Mission District Northern Mexicans known as Nortenos. Chino's murder game and heart helped him quickly rise through the ranks, becoming the Top Soldado or top soldier. He answered to and received orders from Monster, who was an N-Sol and number one in the chain of command of the entire gang.

Lil' Dooka put his Glock 21 back on his waist and grabbed the phone off the sink after washing his hands. Before leaving the bathroom, he lit a Blue Nile-scented incense. By the time he opened the front door shirtless and still rubbing his stomach, Chino was standing with his back to the door scanning the block. He turned around when he heard Lil' Dooka open the front door.

"Damn, fool, what took you so long to open the door?" Chino screwed his face up at Lil' Dooka.

"Nigga, I told yo' ass I was taking a shit. You thought I was lying to you or something. Ain't nobody tell yo' ass to slide through without calling anyway." Lil' Dooka mugged Chino back as he stepped aside to let him in.

"Yeah, yeah, fool, stop complaining and get this money."

The sound of those words brought music to Lil' Dooka's ears. He was always all smiles when it was time to get some dough.

"That's what's up, nigga. What you need? 'Cause I know you didn't drive yo' ass all the way over here for some small shit." Lil' Dooka led Chino over to the dining room table.

"We throwing a little get together in the hood tonight. So, I'mma need a nice little party mixture. You know, a good variety of shit for the hoes to choose from." Chino sat down, ready to see what was good.

"Brah, you talking variety, I got some Instagrams, some Mac Dres, and Facebooks as far as them Smackers go. I just got some fire ass Molly the other day that will have them hoes on like shit. Got some bars and a few perks left too." Lil'

Dooka grabbed a Michael Jordan shoe box and sat it on the table.

"Since a nigga 'bout to snatch a bunch of shit, I know them prices gotta be flexible like Bow Flex."

"You already know." Lil' Dooka set a nice display on the table for Chino to look at.

"Brah, you still fuck wit' lean too?" Chino asked, just remembering that Lil' Dooka sometimes be having his hands on some good syrup.

"I got a few bricks I think. Some of that good hi-tech."

"You already know I'mma need at least two bricks of that shit. Matter of fact, pour up an ounce. It's all on me, homie." Chino pulled out two knots of hundreds.

"My nigga, say less." Lil' Dooka got up and walked to the refrigerator. He grabbed two bricks of Hi-Tech and a brick of that Wock. Even though Chino was offering to share some of his Hi-Tech with Lil' Dooka, Lil' Dooka only fucked with that Wock.

After grabbing two bottles of one liter Sprite Remix, he poured an ounce in both bottles and walked back into the dining room and handed one of the Sprite bottles to Chino. "Here, nigga. I appreciate the gesture, but this one's on me."

"Fa'sho, fool, good looking. What's up in here?" Chino began tilting the bottle back and forth, mixing the concoction.

"Come on, my nigga, you already know what I sip on," Lil' Dooka told him while doing the exact same thing to his bottle. "You figure out what you wanna do yet?"

"Yeah, homie, I'm thinking about a Big Face of each," Chino told him.

Lil' Dooka quickly did the math in his head. Then he adjusted some numbers and told Chino, "I'll tell you what, shoot me nine racks for everything and I'mma throw you two hunnid more Facebooks and this." He grabbed a half ounce of powdered coke (cocaine) and tossed it on the table.

Chino's face lit up. He knew that just the two bricks of Hi-Tech and one hundred Oxys alone was at nine grand. In essence, Lil' Dooka just cut him a deal, saving him about two bands. He happily counted out nine stacks of ten one-hundred-dollar bills while sipping his Sprite. While Chino did that, Lil' Dooka got his order ready for him. By the time Chino left, he was already starting to feel the effects of the Lean.

After locking the door behind Chino, Lil' Dooka went right back in the restroom to take another shit.

***

When Chino pulled up to the spot, he was already on like shit, and Monster could tell. The powder coke that Lil' Dooka had given was straight fish scale. Chino couldn't remember the last time that he'd snorted some coke as good as the shit Lil' Dooka gave him. After leaving Lil' Dooka's spot, Chino found a spot to pull over and take a one on one of the coke. He had to because the potency of the Hi-Tech was more than he was ready for.

The coke was so good it brought him back instantly. Chino rushed home to take a mean shit, shower, and change clothes in preparation for the party. In Chino's mind, it was only given that he finished off his bottle of lean and snorted a good two grams of the coke while he got ready. Even though he was on like shit, Chino was still on point. The ladder hanging out the ass of his Glock .27 was testament to that.

"What's up, big homie?" Chino greeted Monster as he walked up to the killer.

"Shit, from the looks of it, you, homie. Chino, you high as fuck, homie," Monster told his number one soldia.

"Fuck, big homie. You know it ain't a party unless I slide thru this bitch with the party treats. That fool Lil' Dooka hit me wit' some shit that's gonna have this muthafucka popp'n!" Chino felt like a "Rock-Star" with his black Billionaire Boys Club Jeans, BBC shirt, and Nike Foamposites on his feet.

"It's all good, fool, 'cause we trynna have a good time to-night, but just make sure you're on your shit, fool. I don't give a fuck if it is the homies tonight. I still want fools to be on point. So, make sure you tell Casper and the rest of the little homies what I said," Monster barked out.

It was Monster's job to enforce shit and to keep all the young homies in line. He took pride in what he did, and he ruled his camp with an iron first. He wasn't the type of homie to just delegate and bark orders. Monster stayed in the trenches with the soldiers and because of that, his men both loved and respected him. But they loved and respected Chino just a little bit more. To them, Chino was the young, wild, and hungry homeboy just like them. Because of this, they could relate to him. Which was why they often listened to his big ideas and dreams.

"It's all good, big homie. I'll make sure I hit them fools up and let them all know what time it is. Don't worry, big homie, I got you. But what's up, though, fool? You trynna get faded or what?" Chino gave Monster a look like *muthafucka I know you do*.

"You know, homie, let me get a taste of that perico (Span-ish for coke) and a couple of those pills." Monster wasn't one of your typical get-high cats, but he would occasionally snort on a little cocaine and pop ecstasy. Chino smiled as he dug through his sock of goodies, pulling out ten of the Mac Dres and passed them to Monster. Monster immediately popped two of the pills in his mouth and dry swallowed them. Chino dumped a small pile of cocaine onto the table. The noise out-side became louder, but they ignored it because the homies were a rowdy bunch.

Chino made four neat lines right on the table. He passed Monster the straw that he had on him. "Here, big homie, you do the honors."

"Si, mon gracias." Monster grabbed the straw, leaned down, and snorted two lines. The cocaine hit him instantly. It

35

was cool to his nostrils, which immediately became numb. "Si mon."

Monster extended his hand out to hand Chino the straw. As Chino got ready to snort the dope, Casper came running into the house. "Say, fools! That fool Trucho is beating the shit out of Weto. Y'all better stop him before he kills that fool!"

Chino looked up at the intrusion. After hearing what Casper just said, Chino handed the straw to Monster. "Here, big homie, I'll take care of these fools. You knock this down."

Monster thought briefly about it. He wanted to discipline the two idiots for disrespecting his spot like that. However, he liked the initiative of Chino, plus, lil' homie could indeed handle things. So, he accepted the straw and let Chino handle the dispute, while he took care of the remaining two lines.

Chino raced out of the house with Casper on his heels. When he got outside, Chino saw Trucho indeed had Weto in the corner of the yard up against the gate, beating the shit out of him. He noticed a few more homies had shown up while he'd been in the house with Monster. A few of the homegirls had started showing up too. They were all standing around cheering on the fight. Some of the homies got quiet at the sight of Chino coming out of the house.

Chino was fuming with anger. Looking at him, no one could tell. He walked calmly across the yard, paying no one attention, except his target. Ten feet away from the fight, he pulled his gun off his waist. As casual as ever, he walked up behind Trucho and brought the pistol up.

When the blow of the gun crashed against Trucho's head, his knees buckled. The blow wasn't strong enough to do any real damage. That wasn't Chino's objective. He did what he wanted to, and that was to get Trucho's attention in a real way. Regaining some of his strength in his legs, Trucho was ready to fuck up whoever was dumb enough to get involved in his shit. When his eyes met Chino's, all the fight vanished from his eyes.

"Fool, what the fuck is wrong with you muthafuckas? Y'all already know this is not how we get down. Disrespecting the spot like that! Not to mention, you muthafuckas already know what time it is with this red-on-red shit. I advise you two fools to get your shit together before y'all ruin the night and fools start getting DP'd." DP was short for discipline, which something no one in the yard wanted.

"Trucho, now that you done fucked this fool up, take him inside and help him get his shit together. I don't care what started this shit. It better be over!"

No one said a word. Reluctantly, Trucho turned around to Weto, who'd fallen down, to help him up to his feet. Chino turned his back on his younger brother Trucho and scanned the faces looking back at him. These were his people, his familia. They represented all that he had in life and all that he loved. But they were falling off. Over the years, Chino watched their discipline and self-respect decline a lot. But it wasn't their fault. They were all being misled and misguided by the ancient guidance of the old guard, with their ancient teachings, old philosophies, and backward ideas. Not Chino, though. Chino was the voice of a new guard. The face of the people. He would lead his familia back down the right path. He would restore the House of Norte by any means necessary.

When Chino's eyes landed on Smokey, he told homie to take a ride with him, then walked off. Chino never saw the look of respect in Monster's eyes as he watched his protege leave. Nor did Chino see the way Valerie looked at him. His brief display of authority made her pussy wet. She silently told herself that soon, Chino would be hers. Valerie was sure about this. She could feel it in every fiber of her being. She just needed to feel him where she knew he belonged. Between her legs.

Chapter 5

This club was packed tighter than a can of sardines. It would appear everybody and their momma came out tonight to show love and support to the newest star to arise from the ashes of Hell known as East Palo Alto. When Dem Hoodstarz fell off, it seemed no one would carry the torch of success for the city the Bay knew as the Small-Town Cemetery. That was until Skrew came Straight Out of the Mid. When "If I Wasn't Getting Money" ft. Philthy Rich, J Stalin, and Getta Dro hit the scene, muthafuckas knew Skew was about to be a force to reckon with. His new album *Straight Out The Mud Chapter 2: Hustler's Point of View* was straight gasoline and everybody came out to the Bill Graham Pacific Auditorium to show their love and hear the new shit that the streets were raging over.

Regardless of how packed the club was, it wasn't a party until 357 Mobb showed up. The line to get inside the club was down the street and around the corner. It was filled with a few niggaz, but mainly it was scantily dressed women in the line. Everyone trynna to compete with each other to catch the eye of a big fish or an up-and-coming star.

When the 357 Mobb came thru, damn near every female in line almost broke their necks to look at the niggaz who came through the scene looking like celebrities with all the ice that froze the clothes they were wearing. The amount of jewelry they all wore was enough to entice any "jack-boy." Even the little broke wannabe "jack boys" couldn't help but stare in awe of all the jewelry. That was all they did, because everyone knew exactly who the young niggaz wearing all the jewelry were, and nobody wanted to fuck with them.

XO led the way through the packed crowd. His 6'3", 210-pound frame parted the sea of bodies with ease. Those that didn't move on their own accord, he moved with no problem. One look at XO by anyone he moved and they quickly decided it was best not to worry about it. The Bill Graham Auditorium wasn't some hole-in-the-wall. It was the place that the best came to perform at when they came to San Francisco. It wasn't the type of place where one would worry about drama popping off. But in San Francisco, you really never knew.

Although C1ty's head remained straight ahead, his eyes were on constant swivel. He really wasn't the clubbing type. He didn't have time to be among the different clicks of niggaz trying to see who was outshining who in this field or that one. C1ty was focused on getting out of the fucking field all together.

Walking on the side of C1ty, G-Baby knew that her man felt out of place. She could sense his uneasiness in his steps. At nineteen years of age, standing 5'0" and weighing 165 pounds, G-Baby drew the attention of more than a few niggaz with her smooth brown skin and long wavy hair that trailed down her back. She was full-blooded Mexican, but her features were more exotic, like that of a female from South America instead of Central America.

G-baby, whose real name was Genesis, was the quiet wifey type. She was from the hood but far from ghetto. In fact, she was attending the University of San Francisco studying to be an accounting major. She only had another year and a half left before graduating and earning her degree. She loved C1ty more than anyone she'd ever known in life. Although she wasn't a street chick, she didn't have a problem putting it all on the line for her man.

Don and Dell both had their necks on swivel. Yet, they were not looking out for danger. They both were looking across the sea of bodies at all of the beautiful women. Each man looking for his pick of the litter to see who he was taking home for the night. One thing the two brothers shared in common was their taste in women. They both liked wild, ghetto that looked glamorous but acted niggerish. Wes often joked telling his brothers that they loved sophisticated boppers, which was a perfect way of explaining it.

The group made their way to the V.I.P section that was set up and waiting for them. The Bill Graham Auditorium was a huge auditorium. It was once home of the Golden State Warriors. The patrons on the second floor could look out across the entire dance floor. Murda could feel eyes staring at all of them from every direction. He was ready to act a freaking fool if anyone got out of line.

The sound of Shark Montana's voice could be heard coming out of the speakers as the DJ played the song "Right Now" off the new album. Once they finally reached their V.I.P section, C1ty told the waitress to bring cases of D'ussé Bel Aire, the black bottle, and Hennessy to start the night off right.

***

MoMo was sitting to the left side of the club in their own V.I.P with the rest of the Tear It Off click, when the 357 Mobb came walking through like they owned the joint. He didn't know who the niggaz were and didn't give a fuck. The little bitch walking with the group of niggaz was what caught MoMo's attention. She was a bad little muthafucka. As MoMo watched her walk, his eyes took in every single curve that she had under her Better Living jeans. To the big Samoan, G-Baby was a treat he just had to have. He picked up his bottle of Ace of Spades and took a big thirst-quenching swallow. At the same time, he grabbed his dick through his jeans. MoMo made up his mind. Fuck the sucka she was with. Little mama was leaving with him.

"Damn, nigga, you sitting there eye hawking that lil' bitch like she's a fat ass pork chop or something!" 4-Boy leaned over on the couch so MoMo could hear him. When he did, the lights performed a matrix show as they bounced off of 4-Boy's '4 Ever Greezy' diamond chain.

"I don't know about no pork chop, nigga, but a nigga can't lie, lil' mama fo'real looking like something a nigga trynna eat on, though," MoMo replied before another swallow of his drink.

"Oh. Excuse me?" the little thick chick that MoMo had been spitting game to before G-Baby walked in, asked with an attitude. "You just gonna sit there and say that fuck shit, like a bitch ain't still sitting here or some shit?"

"Bitch, I don't know who the fuck you think you talking to. I don't give a fuck if you sitting there or if you ain't. Bitch, I'mma say what the fuck I wanna say whenever the fuck I wanna say it. If you don't like it, bitch, you can do it moving." MoMo looked at the white chick like she was special ed retarded.

She was a bad little snow bunny with some phat double D tits that had bullets for nipples. The nipples stuck so far out of her Better Living white tube top that it was a wonder they didn't burst right through the fabric. She didn't have much of an ass, but on her 5'5" frame, the little ass that she did have looked good enough. It was her fire-engine-red hair that caught MoMo's attention as it flowed like the Nile River down to her ass. MoMo loved a chick with long hair. It drove him crazy.

"You're not about to sit there and do that punk shit in front of me like I'm some kind of busted bitch—"

"Amber, girl, stop tripping. You know niggaz gone be niggaz. Let that nigga do him, bitch, while you do you," Jackie, Amber's roommate, cut her off.

Jackie was all up on Reco next to Amber and MoMo's left side. In fact, it was because of Jackie that they were in V.I.P. with the TIO click in the first place, and she didn't need Amber fucking that up. Jackie had been checking for Reco for a cool minute. So, when he told the waitress to bring her and Amber to the V.I.P. section, Jackie decided she would make the best out of her chance to get with Reco.

"Bitch, fuck that! Jackie, you might be okay with niggaz disrespecting you, but not me. It's way too much dick in the world for me to put up with that shit!" Amber couldn't believe

Jackie would side with some dick over her. That was some typical shit from a sack chaser. How could she expect anything more than that from her roommate?

"Bitch, I'm not the one getting disrespected. That's yo' high sadity ass. Don't get fucked up!" Jackie fired back. Amber was always trying to act like her shit didn't stink and Jackie was tired of it.

"Fuck this shit!" Amber shot back. Amber knew she looked good. *I can get any guy in the club,* she told herself. She didn't have to put up with this. "And, Jackie, since you wanna side with this muthafucka, fuck you too!"

"Bye, bitch!" Jackie called out as Amber stormed off.

Lil' Dooka just shook his head. He knew his brother MoMo was a wild nigga. At the same time, Lil' Dooka thought the little white bitch overreacted. At the end of the day, he didn't give a fuck. His attention was really on the little bitch that was sitting on his lap. The shit she was talking in his ear had Lil' Dooka ready to fuck her brains out right there in V.I.P. He pulled two Tesla triple stacks out of his pocket. He popped the first one. The second he placed on his tongue and passed it to the little bitch when he kissed her. Alexis was already on fire. Her pussy had been wet from the moment she sat down on Lil' Dooka's lap. She felt the E-pill he had on his tongue when he kissed her and hungrily sucked it off, knowing it would send her pussy into overdrive.

Suddenly, the lights all dimmed and everybody grew silent in anticipation of the show starting. The sound of the automatic rifle fire erupted through the speakers. When the gunshots stopped echoing in the speakers, a woman's voice announced, "We interrupt your schedule show to bring to you this emergency news broadcast. The Alameda Sheriff's Department along with the US Marshalls and the Federal Bureau of Investigation have issued a nationwide manhunt for a Marcus Greene for multiple murders and multiple attempted murders.

"The chargers stem from a shooting incident that occurred on October 7, 2020, in the city of Hayward. It is alleged that two rival street gangs, the Decepticons and The Taliban Gang, who have been involved in a long street war, had a deadly shootout that left eleven people dead and seven more wounded. Officials tell us that, supposedly, Marcus Greene, a founding member of the Taliban Gang, and members of the Decepticons got into an altercation in the club that led to one of the members of the Decepticons being hospitalized for a fractured jaw. The altercation is said to have spilled out onto the streets where Marcus Greene, known as Shark Montana, and his Taliban Gang opened fire…" The pre-recorded news broadcast was interrupted by the sounds of a man's deep voice. "Don't let that bother you, bitch!" Right after that remark, the sound of Skrew's song "Be Cool" featuring Shark Montana came over the speakers.

"I heard these niggaz talking loud. Dey betta be cool/cuz I don't wanna show 'em how I make this chop move/We focus on some big moves/so we ain't worried 'bout chou niggaz over there so don't worry 'bout what we do!"

The chorus had everybody in the house grooving in their seats to the flow and the rhythm of the beat. The easy-going vibe was short lived. Once the lights cut back on, the entire club went bonkers, ape shit crazy! All the women were screaming. The ones who were seated, jumped out of their seats. Even the gangstas came to their feet and howled, giving their support and showing their respect for what they were witnessing. Standing among a sea of about 30 Taliban soldiers all clad in black and grey Better Living army fatigue, was Shark Montana, standing tall like the true general he was, fearless.

"I said somebody tell that funky cunt hoe/Don't let that bother you!" he roared into the microphone.

"Don't let that bother you, bitch!" the crowd shouted.

"Saut-te-tey," Shark Montana called out after a chuckle just before opening up his verse.

"I hear these niggaz talking loud, dey betta be coo/'cuz I don't wanna show 'em how I make this chop move/we focus on some big moves/but this shit gets kinda hard when yo' face is on the news/I'm in too deep so I can't lose/so I gotta think smarter/make sure my next move be my best move..." Screens lit up with giant screen shots of his FBI wanted photo.

Skrew was on stage right next to Shark Montana with a bottle of lean in one hand and a microphone in his other. The moment was magical. The women were going crazy just at the mere sight of the tall, dark-skinned, skinny nigga from the Bay Area's most wanted jungle. Skrew was happy to have his big homie on the stage with him right by his side. It was Skrew who was behind everybody all wearing Better Living apparel tonight. Skrew was trying to get Shark Montana to realize that they would always be street niggaz but were now bigger than the streets.

Chapter 6

The Bill Graham Pacific Auditorium had never been so electrifying. The energy level was through the roof. While Skrew and Shark Montana spit their verses to "Be Cool," Getta Dro grabbed a mic and blazed his verse. A commotion drew everyone's attention to the left side of the stage just in time to see The Live Wire Camp storming the stage in preparation for Philthy Rich and J. Stalin to help Skrew and Getta Dro take the crowd back to 2016 with their number one single "If I Wasn't Getting Money."

C1ty couldn't lie, he was happy the family had decided to come out and lend their support and enjoy the night. Everything was popping and everybody was in a good mood. Even with all the good times that everyone was having, C1ty just couldn't shake the feeling that they made a mistake by coming to the event. Something just felt out of place to him, and since he couldn't quite put his finger on what it was, he didn't like it.

G-Baby noticed C1ty hadn't relaxed all night. She tried to help loosen him up with a couple of lap dances and personal erotic jokes she whispered in his ear. Realizing it wasn't working, she decided that she would see if he wanted to call it a night, but first, she had to go to the lady's room.

"De'Mario, baby, I have to go to the little girl's room. I was hoping that maybe you could take me home once I get back, because I am not feeling too well," she leaned over and told him in his ear.

At the sound of hearing G-Baby say she wasn't well, C1ty took his eyes off of the room and focused on his soon-to-be wife.

"What's wrong, baby? Come on, I'll walk you to the bathroom," he told her in a voice that showed his concern.

"No, it's okay, baby. I can make it to the ladies room by myself. I would just like you to take me home once I'm finished. My stomach is just upset and I think I should lay down."

"Alright, baby. It's all good. We'll get up out of here as soon as you get back." C1ty kissed his baby on the cheek. Just a small show of affection to let her know he loved her.

When G-Baby got up, C1ty followed her as far as he could with his eyes before she was soon swallowed up and blended in with the sea of bodies. When she was out of sight, C1ty got CJ's attention and informed his second in command that he was going to leave early and take G-Baby home.

"What's good, Brah-Brah? You want me to send somebody with y'all to make sure everything's, everything?" CJ asked his little cousin while his hand rubbed across the booty on the lil' chick sitting in his lap.

"Naaw, it's good, my nigga. You know the nigga Plies say *I keep that Body Guard on me*." C1ty patted his waist in reference to the big .357 that he had for tough niggaz and dumb ass niggaz alike.

CJ laughed at his cousin, said alright, then turned his attention back to the big ole booty in his lap.

After performing "If I Wasn't Getting Money," Philthy Rich performed one of his new songs off his upcoming album. Afterwards, Stalin decided to take the crowd back in the day as he and the rest of the Wire performed, "Don't Tell Me Who Telling," off their first mixtape, *We the Wire*.

Halfway through the song, C1ty realized G-Baby had been gone for quite some time. With her telling him that she didn't feel well, he became concerned. He didn't say anything to anybody. C1ty just got up and went to check on his baby. Without him saying a word, the moment he walked off, XO was right behind him.

***

The moment he saw the little cutie get up and walk out the other V.I.P section by herself, MoMo knew it was the moment he had been waiting for. The chance for him to do his thang and pop his collar. From the direction she was headed, he knew that she had to be on her way to the bathroom. He picked up his bottle of Moet and made his way over in that direction. He thought to himself that he would catch her little thick ass as she was coming back out of the bathroom. The Moet was his third bottle of the champagne. It wasn't enough to have the big Samoan drunk. Although, the shots of Hennessy that he'd taken added just enough liquor power to have him on a slight tilt. He walked like it too.

G-Baby was relieved to finally exit the restroom. It seemed like she would never get out it was so many women inside. The line just to get inside of the restroom was about a five-minute wait. After she finished peeing, G-Baby didn't dare attempt to fight her way to a sink amongst the thirsty hyenas that crowded the mirrors, desperately trying to fix themselves in hope of snagging a juicy piece of steak or a baller.

She was making her way back across the club when a huge Samoan stepped in her path.

"God damn, little cutie, I don't know where you're in a rush to, but a nigga trynna get a small moment of your time before you disappear, just in case you're returning back to Heaven." MoMo looked down at G-Baby and bit his bottom lip as he swayed just barely.

"The compliment was sweet, thank you. But I'm sorry, I'm not interested in any conversation or companionship. You might want to use your smoothness on one of these other ladies." G-Baby was as polite as she could be, but she didn't need for C1ty to see some nigga trying to holla at her. C1ty had a mean jealous streak.

MoMo wasn't one to give up easily. He stepped a little closer to G-Baby. "Naaw, little mama. Why would I want to waste my time talking to a runner-up when I'm sure that I'm

49

already talking to Ms. First Place? Ma, ain't nobody in here fucking with you."

G-Baby took a step back, put off by his aggressiveness. Although he was saying some good shit, he was saying it to the wrong chick.

"Look, I'm flattered and all, but I came here with my dude and he's not going to like it one bit if he sees you pressing me. Now I'm trying to do you a favor and tell you to keep it pushing before he do," she said with just a slight attitude. MoMo was taking a drink from his bottle, so she tried to sidestep him as she was saying this.

"What, bitch?" MoMo felt disrespected by the way G-Baby was brushing him off. And he damn sure wasn't feeling a threat coming from no bitch. He blocked her path again and reached around, grabbing a handful of her juicy ass. "Bitch, I'm not worried about that bitch-ass nigga that you came in here with or them bitch-ass niggaz that are with him. I know that lil' skinny nigga ain't hitting dis shit right. You need to get some of this fat USO dick!" G-Baby smacked MoMo's hand off her ass.

"Bitch ass nigga, don't be putting yo' muthafuck'n hands on me! I'm not your bitch. You faggot ass nigga!" Before MoMo could respond, she reached up and slapped the dog shit out of him.

The alcohol had MoMo's reflexes a little too slow. Therefore, he wasn't able to dodge the blow. Being caught off guard caused MoMo to drop the bottle of Moet that he was drinking from. Full of rage, he cocked his right arm all the way back so he could knock the Holy Shit out of the little stuck-up bitch.

G-Baby tensed up, closing her eyes in preparation for the blow that never came. While her eyes were closed, she silently wished she would have let C1ty walk her to the restroom. When she opened her eyes, C1ty was standing over MoMo, who was down on one knee. G-Baby never saw MoMo stagger before dropping from the force of C1ty busting him upside his head with a bottle of Bel Aire he had in his hand.

Powerful as it was, the blow was not strong enough to knock MoMo out. The angry Samoan shook the dizzy spell from his head and growled like a full-grown grizzly bear as he climbed to his feet. MoMo didn't hesitate to get off in C1ty's ass. He hit C1ty with a two-piece jab followed by a bone-crushing left hook to the jaw. The blow by the big Samoan shook the slim, 165-pound, C1ty to his core. The only thing that kept C1ty on his feet was the nigga that he stumbled into.

As C1ty tried to shake the stars out of his vision, MoMo advanced on him. The people in the immediate surrounding area who became aware of the fight moved out of the way to give the two niggaz fighting some room. MoMo threw a right then a left to C1ty's body. He prepared to knock the little skinny nigga out, when it felt like he got kicked in the side of the head by a mule.

MoMo stumbled backward, wondering what happened. He barely had time to see the large, muscular frame of XO come into his vision before everything went black. XO gave him a two-piece combo so vicious that it knocked him smoothly on his ass. It was a left hook followed by a devastating right uppercut.

After knocking MoMo out, XO turned his attention to C1ty to make sure he was okay. Lil' Dooka had other plans, though. Seeing the commotion from V.I.P. , he bounced up and ran to MoMo's aid. It was a waste of time. Lil' Dooka caught XO on the side of the jaw with an old-school dope-fiend haymaker. The problem for Lil' Dooka was the punch didn't do shit to XO. Lil' Dooka was a shooter, not a fighter. It pissed off XO, who commenced to beating the shit out of Lil' Dooka. The only thing that saved Lil' Dooka was the chaos that erupted once both groups inside of the V.I.P. section realized what was going on.

The brawl ended up lasting almost ten minutes before security was able to get things back under control. In order to get things peaceful, one of the groups had to get kicked out. As fate should have it, that group was Lil' Dooka and his TIO click. That decision would haunt the streets of San Francisco for years to come.

Lil' Dooka wasn't the type of nigga to take a L (a loss). He had no plans on tonight being any different. As security escorted them out of the club, his mind was made up that he was going to air this bitch out. "Dooka! Dooka!"

He looked in the direction the voice that was calling him from. It was hard to see with one of his eyes swollen. He concentrated and was able to make out Gabby's face emerging from the crowd. Gabby ran up to and into her man's arms. The sight of his swollen and bruised face brought tears to her eyes.

"Dooka, what happened, baby?" Gabby was scared and frantic. She had never seen him look like this.

"Nothing, just bullshit. What are you doing here?" he asked her, embarrassed that his woman was seeing him all fucked up and shit.

"I thought I would come and surprise you. I had no—"

He cut her off. "Well, you gotta get out of here. Now's not a good time. Shit's about to get ugly, and I don't need you up in here." Nosey bastards were all up in their shit. So, he pulled her off to the side, away from listening ears.

"Baby, I didn't drive. I had Teresa drop me off. I was expecting to go home with you."

By now, they'd started walking in the direction of their vehicles. The entire TIO clique was pissed the fuck off. The only thing on their minds as they angrily made their way to the parking lot was bodying some shit. The people that were left in line could tell some shit was about to hit the fan just by looking at the angry faces on the group of niggaz walking by them. The smart ones decided to cut their evening short and walk out of the line back to their cars and leave.

He had to think for a minute. Lil' Dooka had to get Gabby safe as soon as possible. He looked around and finally decided on a plan. "Hey, 4-Boy!" he called out to 4-Boy, who was busy telling T.G. what he was about to do.

4-Boy came over to Lil' Dooka, who was now standing by the driver's side of his Mustang. "What's up, brotha?"

"Brah, look, I need to get Gabby up out of here. You know it's drill time, but she can't be here. Brotha, I need you to do that for me." 4-Boy wanted to protest and tell Lil' Dooka fuck no, but the look on Lil' Dooka's face left no room for debate.

On top of that, 4-Boy knew that if it was him that just got his ass, kicked he would want his revenge, no doubt. Disappointed that he wasn't going to be able to body some shit, he grabbed the keys to the Mustang from Lil' Dooka. Gabby tried to protest out of fear of what Dooka was about to do. Yet, she knew better than to go against him at a time like this. Especially when he was with his brothas. So, she reluctantly did what Lil' Dooka said and climbed in the car with 4-Boy.

When Lil' Dooka turned around to face his brotha, his boyish, innocent features that drove the women crazy were gone. The look on his face resembled a pure demon.

Chapter 7

After the commotion, things went back to normal inside of the club. After all, it was only a minor scuffle. Everybody inside the club had witnessed far worse than that. So once Shark Montana yelled "Don't let that bother you!" into the microphone and the beat dropped, people went right back to doing their thang and enjoying the show.

That was except for the 357 Mobb. The V.I.P. section was filled with electric energy. The negative kind.

"Blood, I'm telling you that was them Tear It Off niggaz! I know that was that bitch ass lil' nigga Dooka. I'd know his face anywhere! I'm telling you, them niggaz been thinking that they them niggaz ever since that bitch ass nigga beat that big case. Nigga, on God, we need to slide through them niggaz shit and wake their game up!" Wes was pissed off, amped up, and drunk. A real fucked up combination.

"TIO? You talking 'bout them faggot ass Sunnydale niggaz?" Don had heard the name Tear It Off (TIO) a while back when one of his niggaz was telling him about the inner beef Sunnydale had going on between the top and the bottom. Or the Four and the Law, as they referred to it.

"Yeah, that's who the fuck I'm talking 'bout! Lil' Dooka from The Four. One of them Blythedale niggaz. That's why he was helping that USO nigga. Brah, they all Blythedale niggaz." Wes reached for the bottle of Remy that was on the table in front of him.

"I don't give a fuck who they were or where them little niggaz is from. Don't nobody touch this muthafuck'n family. Niggaz already know. I'm on that same shit Wes is on, nigga, it's drill time!" Dell's light-skinned complexion had a dark tint to it. His skin always took on a darker tone whenever his anger rose.

G-Baby was tending to a bruised and sore C1ty. She was scared as hell but was trying not to show it. She knew exactly

De'Kari

who Lil' Dooka was. Everybody did. After the shooting at the mall, his face had been on every news channel in California. She didn't want C1ty getting into it with anybody, let alone someone crazy and brazen enough to have a shootout in the middle of a mall in broad daylight.

C1ty was fuming. He remained quiet for so long while everyone talked and carried on because he was using every ounce of restraint to remain calm. "First off, y'all need to kill all that chatter all out in the open like this. What's already understood ain't gotta be spoken. What we're gonna do is get the fuck out of here and head to the spot. Once we're there, we gone figure out our next move."

Murda already knew what the next move was. Wes was right. It was time to body some shit. A disrespect like that wasn't to be tolerated. Especially not in the jungles of San Francisco. C1ty was right, now wasn't the time nor the place. More importantly, there wasn't shit to talk about except strategy. Therefore, Murda said nothing as the group made its way out of the V.I.P., headed for the door.

The moment they walked out of the club and into the chilly night air, C1ty knew something was wrong. That fucked up feeling he'd had all night was now screaming at him. He pulled the long .357 off his hip as he scanned the night, looking for any sign of danger. Picking up on his cousin's mood, CJ came off the hip as well, while searching for danger. Something in the dark off to his right side caught CJ's attention. There was movement deep inside the shadows, so he turned his attention to the shadow.

At that moment, an all-black Dodge Charger came racing around the corner to their left. Everyone's attention quickly shifted in that direction. Only then did CJ realize his mistake. The shots erupted from the dark shadows first. From the exact spot CJ had been searching with his eyes. A second later, the inside of the Dodge Charger lit up from the muzzle flash of several automatics firing from multiple windows at the same time.

G-Baby cried out as bullets barreled into her side, tearing her out of C1ty's grip and sending her body crashing into the wall behind her. Murda was the first from their side to open fire, grateful for his decision earlier to give the bouncer a thousand-dollar tip not to search any of them when they arrived at the club. Now the compact 9mm that he pulled from his waistline added to the chorus of gunfire as he sent shots at the Dodge Charger.

The 357 Mobb was under attack from both sides. CJ quickly slapped a speed reloader into his cannon. He was able to pinpoint one of the shooters in the alley from the muzzle flash of his gun. Instantly, CJ sent his mini missiles to that exact location. The sound of Nardy screaming out, let CJ know that he hit his target.

When G-Baby cried out, C1ty instantly looked her way. The sight of her little body slamming against the wall killed his soul. He ran to shield her body from further bullets and received two hot fuck yous in his back as a reward. After dropping C1ty with two shots, Lil' Dooka looked over across the alley at Bubz, who was laying on his back fighting a losing battle against death as blood invaded his lungs.

Bullet after bullet riddled the Dodge Charger. Whoever had been shooting from the backseat was no longer returning fire. Only the passenger continued to send mini messengers of death into the night. Police sirens could be heard, yet the shootout continued.

As another rally of shots riddled the Charger, the driver finally decided to speed off. Seeing his big brother and leader drop from the two slugs that ripped into him, Wes lost it! He raced across the darkened street into the mouth of the alley, where he found Bubz barely clutching on to life. Wes stood over Bubz with no remorse and pulled the trigger of the big .357. There was no sign of the second shooter. Wes silently begged for there to be another shooter somewhere. But there wasn't. Lil' Dooka took off out the back of the alley moments before the Dodge Charger sped off. Wes turned around, leaving Bubz's dead body with a head that resembled a smashed pumpkin.

Wes jogged back across the street. Several bodies laid sprawled across the sidewalk. Nine of which were pedestrians who were foolish enough to still be in the line waiting admittance into the show. The cries from the injured joined the now loud sirens of the coming police.

"We gotta get the fuck outta here!" CJ called out to his family, the bullet hole in his shoulder making him grimace as he yelled. "Make sure we get brah's gun. XO, stay with brah and Baby. Everybody else, let's go, we got shit to do!"

None of the remaining relatives wanted to leave C1ty and G-Baby. They all wanted to be there for them, but they all knew the consequences if they did. Reluctantly, every man fled, scattering in different directions, and merged in with the thousands of shadows that lurked in the night.

***

When C1ty dove, the only thing on his mind was protecting G-Baby. The team, the family, his safety. None of that mattered to him. He never felt the bullets that tore through his body. As he crashed into G-Baby, both of their bodies landed on the sidewalk with his body on top protecting hers. It was the feeling of hot liquid flowing out of his body that told C1ty he had been shot. His blood oozing out of the bullet holes felt like acid seeping out of his body. The pain brought tears to his eyes. Even in all of his pain, he could only think about G-Baby being shot and pray that she was okay. The last thing C1ty heard before passing out was CJ barking out orders. The last thing he thought was, *Lord, please protect my baby!*

***
(A few hours later)

58

The twenty-three-year-old general had been second in command ever since the family all got together. His role had always been C1ty's right hand man. Now he was forced to be thrown into lead command by circumstance. CJ tilted the pint of Hennessy for a full ten seconds, gulping almost half the bottle at once. He screwed his face up. Not from the alcohol, but the pain in his shoulder as Tiny cleansed the hole the bullet left as it entered the front and exited out the back.

It was hard concentrating on ignoring the pain, listening to everything being said, thinking about his loved ones laid up in the hospital, and trying to figure out what to do next. Yet, the young general was doing it.

"Brah, y'all looking at this shit all wrong. Nigga, I'm not being emotional or reckless, I'm being strategical. The same way C1ty would be. After what the fuck just happened, the last thing that them bitch ass niggaz is going to expect is us sliding through wet'n some shit tonight. They know for a fact that they hit G-Baby, and I'm sure they know they got brah too. Them niggaz right now think we at the hospital all crying and shit like bitches, 'cause that's what most muthafuckas would do in this situation!" Wes knew he was making sense. He just couldn't understand why they didn't see shit right.

Don and Dell both thought the smart thing to do was to kick back and analyze the situation while things died down a little. Wes wanted to do the opposite. He figured they should slide over to Sunnydale tonight and light that bitch up. Killing Bubz didn't do shit to quench his thirst for revenge. C1ty was his favorite brother, and Wes was ready to teach muthafuckas a lesson about fucking with his people.

"I don't give a fuck when we move. All I know is I'm 'bout to seriously murk some shit!" XO leaned over the plate on the coffee table and snorted the two lines of Belushi that were waiting for him. He tilted his head back and allowed the powdered cocaine and heroin mix to run straight to his brain.

CJ had heard enough. He knew Dell and Don were both trying to be cautious. He couldn't do nothing but respect that. However, what Wes was saying was logical as fuck. The TIO niggaz wouldn't expect for them to try and bust a doll tonight. Niggaz weren't really moving like that. He looked across the room at a quiet Murda. CJ already knew what his older cousin was thinking. He could read his body language all too easily. The smell of Peanut Butter Breath Cookies that he was smoking had the entire room in a peanut-buttery haze.

"How much longer you gone take wit' this shit, Tiny?" CJ's mind was made up. It was time to ride. The wound in his shoulder was now just a fucking nuisance.

"I'm going as fast as I can, CJ, damn. Just stay still, baby, and it shouldn't be much longer than five more minutes!"

"Aight, then check it out. Don, I understand the importance of what you and Dell are saying, but I think Wes is right on this one. The last thing them niggaz expecting is for us to bring it to they ass tonight. I think that's exactly what we should do. Murda, what you think?" CJ looked at Murda, waiting for a response.

The look that Murda gave him told the entire room what Murda thought. It was Murda Season.

"Since XO already said it's whatever, that's the vote. As soon as you get finished, Tiny, I need you to go by General and check on Baby and brah. The police shouldn't give you a hard time. The rest of us gone work this shit out as soon as she leaves. Believe me, though, we gone burn this bitch tonight."

Looking at Tiny's 5'1", 123-pound frame with her innocent features like her big, dewy eyes, no one would expect her to hang out with a crowd like this. She graduated from USF with her nurse practitioner's license and was the assistant practitioner at St. Luke's Hospital. Her baby face features made her look nineteen instead of her twenty-nine years. Growing up in Double Rock herself, she'd been a part of the family her entire life. Still, she wasn't family. Therefore, CJ wasn't going to talk in front of her. He knew C1ty wouldn't, so he wasn't.

After Tiny finished up stitching CJ's shoulder and left, the Mobb sat in the living room for fifteen more minutes going over everything. When they were done, it was time to remind muthafuckas what the Mobb was about.

Chapter 8

No one spoke a word in either car as the two vehicles drove southwest along Bayshore Blvd. The three killers in the all-black Charger followed close behind the two killers in the all-black Challenger. The two-car caravan turned right onto Sunnydale Ave. The two vehicles resembled nothing more than movable digits attached to the fist of the darkness they called night.

Down at the other end of the street, twelve niggaz were hanging out, smoking, and talking shit. It was a normal night for the niggaz from the bottom of Sunnydale, also known as the Low. The Low was at the bottom of Sunnydale Projects and The Four was at the top. They were different sides of the same project that were at war with each other. A sad fact of reality of life inside of San Francisco.

Lil' Baby, one of the notorious niggaz from the Low, was rolling a Backwood of Gushers. As he brought the blunt to his lips to seal it, he spotted the two black vehicles driving up Sunnydale Ave with tinted windows.

"Watch them muthafuckas coming up the street." The moment Lil' Baby called out the warning, all twelve niggaz' hands went toward their different weapons. On point and ready.

The wildest nigga out the clique was a light-skinned, thirty-two-year-old nigga with long dreads that hung down his back. His name was Kino, but everyone called him 'Kino The Great!' Kino picked up the baby AR-15 with a scope off of the trunk of his BMW M4 CS and looked through the scope. Kino was ready to let the mini missiles inside of the choppa fly.

Something wasn't right. Kino had been in the field since a little nigga. Over the years, he learned to listen to his instincts. Looking at the two vehicles, he didn't get the feel of a threat. No doubt the vehicles looked smirkish the way they were coming back-to-back. However, they were moving too fast. Kino knew A-lot wasn't their destination.

"Them niggaz ain't coming for us. Whoever they 'bout to slide on, it ain't us," he called out as he lowered his deadly weapon.

Even though most of his niggaz knew Kino knew his shit, they weren't about to take no chances. So, as the 357 Mobb drove by A-lot, there were at least eight different guns pointed at them. Once the cars drove by, most of the niggaz in the Low went right back to what they were doing, while a couple still wondered what the niggaz in the cars were up to.

Fifty something seconds later, they received their answer when the peaceful dark night was awakened by the sound of automatic gunfire. It was then that Kino realized where he knew the two vehicles from. He was over at Two Jacks three weeks ago when XO and Murda pulled up in the same black Challenger. Kino knew then that it was the Double Rock 357 Mobb niggaz getting off on The Four niggaz. He sat the assault rifle back on top of his car and nodded his head, hoping that they murdered a couple of them niggaz.

***

(A couple of minutes before)

Even though Lil' Dooka was sore as fuck from the ass kicking he received from XO, he sat in the small project room smoking. The satisfaction of dropping a couple of bodies on the other side took his mind off the pain. He'd been on the phone now for almost twenty minutes trying to calm Gabby down and assure her that everything was alright.

"Gabby, babe, listen to me, fuck! I'm telling you, ma, that it's okay. Damn, it wasn't nothing but a fight."

"But Dooka, the news is saying that there was some kind of big shootout afterwards right in front of the club. Supposedly, somebody died and everything." Gabby was sitting at home going crazy.

She just finished watching the news coverage of the shootout at the club. The moment the coverage began, her heart started racing. All she could think about was something happening to Dooka.

"Babe, I told you we left when you left, so you should've known there was no way we could be a part of that."

"You should've known there's no way we could've been a part of that!" his little nineteen-year-old cousin, Nardy, mocked him openly. "Nigga, you sounding like a straight little bitch right now explaining yo'self to that bitch!" Nardy laughed hysterically at this own joke.

Lil' Dooka ignored Nardy's little ignorant ass and went right on trying to calm Gabby down.

Nardy was a real problem child. A rare breed of demon. At the age of six, he witnessed his first homicide right underneath his bedroom window. Two niggaz had gotten into an argument over a female. The big dude beat the shit out of the little one. Unfortunately for the big dude, the little dude had a gun on him and pulled it out and shot him. That was life in the projects.

The police took almost an hour to respond to the shooting. Again, that was life in the projects. Even once the police arrived, the dead body laid sprawled out on the ground for hours. Little Nardy stared at the body the entire time. Fascinated. He had seen death before, so it wasn't new to him. However, he was still too young to fully grasp the concept of death. Yet, he was old enough to understand, whatever a gun was, it was powerful enough to stop the big man for good. Nardy watched in amazement as the flies began to swarm around the body. Crawling all on its force, yet the man couldn't even move to get them off of him. He could move no more.

Nardy wanted that kind of power!

He would find it a year later at the age of seven. It was then that he found himself in the position of the little guy getting beat up and picked on by the bigger guy. One day, he watched from his bedroom window as a nigga from the hood ran from the police and tossed a gun that he never found once they caught him. They didn't find it when they came back to search for it because little Nardy had already came and picked it up. He was sitting in his room watching the police search for the gun that he held in his small hands. Later that night, he shot and killed the big bully that had been picking on him, with the same gun. It was then a demon was born.

Over the span of two years, Nardy would kill three more people. Including his mom's abusive boyfriend. One night, after beating Nardy's mom unconscious, the boyfriend went out to the back of the projects to get drunk. Little Nardy found him drunk at the top of Cement Hill. After shooting him with the last four bullets in the gun, Nardy ran and threw the gun away in the dumpster behind the projects. Then he went home, walked to his room, and stared at the dead body for hours, until the coroner finally took it away.

"Bitch, yo' mama gone sound like a little bitch when she run her black ass in here begging me to stop beating yo' ass 'cause you talk too much shit," Lil' Dooka joked as soon as he hung up the phone on Gabby.

"More like she gone be begging me to stop beating you upside yo' shit with this .40." Nardy cracked back as he just finished wiping down his Glock .27.

Nardy glanced out his window in time to see two all-black vehicles pulling up to the bottom of Cement Hill with their lights turned off.

"Them Low niggaz on the Hill!" He quickly tucked the Glock on his waist and reached for the Draco that was lying on his bed.

Lil' Dooka didn't waste any time looking out of the window. He bounced up and pulled his Glock .17 off of his waist as he and Nardy both raced out of the bedroom.

***

"Kill them lights," Murda told Don. They had just passed A-lot and were approaching Cement Hill.

Don did exactly that. The Charger did the same thing, and within seconds, both cars pulled up to the bottom of Cement Hill, and everybody got out strapped and ready!

Murda scanned the area. He was looking for both prey and any potential threat. Sounds of laughter and shit talking drifted in the air. The sounds were coming from the top of that hill. Murda looked over, making eye contact with Don. No words needed to be said. In unison, they proceeded up the Hill. The rest of the Mobb followed.

"Nigga, I don't even know why yo' ass is sitting there lying! As soon as yo' ass felt this wet ass pussy, yo' little dick started erupting like a volcano. A bitch couldn't even whip the pussy on you good because you were cumming so fucking fast!" Everybody died laughing. Marlene was teasing and talking shit to Turk about their little escapade the other day.

Marlene put her hand down in front of her pants acting like she was holding a dick and started making sounds with her mouth like water spitting out of a water hose. They were all hanging out at the top of Cement Hill, chilling and talking shit. It began with them smoking and drinking in memory of Bubz. None of the young savages cried for their fallen folks because they all understood that death was part of the game. Instead, they drank, smoked, and partied to honor Bubz's life. They would not mourn his death.

"Yeah. Yeah. Bitch, you wasn't saying that shit once a nigga got hard again. When a nigga had you bent over beating yo' fucking brains out. Yo' ass was all *Ah! Ah! Turk, wait! Hold up, Turk, you killing a bitch!*" Turk was making all kinds of fuck faces as he imitated the sound of Marlene pleading to him.

"Yeah, bitch, you was running from that dick so much yo' whole fucking head almost went inside a bitch's pussy," Stacy joined in.

"Oh, bitch, I know you ain't talking—" Marlene didn't get the chance to finish her sentence. The .223 that hit her face, knocking the bottom half of her jaw off, prevented that. Her lifeless body flew backward off its feet from the force of the bullet.

T.G. was the first to act out of everybody to respond. He was standing a couple of feet behind Marlene. He caught her body in midair as it was flying backward. He wrapped his left arm around Marlene's lifeless neck, and with his right arm he snatched his .40 Cal off his waist and returned fire. He didn't think twice about using Marlene's body as a shield. The bitch was already dead, so he didn't give a fuck!

When Stacy saw Marlene's body fly backward, she let out a loud scream. The sight of her friend flying backward through the air scared the shit out of Stacy. She didn't know what else to do, so she began running toward the projects.

Reco and MoMo both stood their ground, trading shot for shot with whoever the fuck was shooting at them, but neither of them gave a fuck. They were just trying to take a mutha-fucka's head off.

Turk was pissed the fuck off. He couldn't believe that his gun had jammed on him. He dropped down to one knee and continued to jack off the slide of his cannon, desperately try-ing to unjam the gun. A couple of bullets flew by his head, forcing him to crouch down even lower. While he kept jacking the slide back, all he could think of was how fucked up it would be if he died without having the fucking opportunity to get off one shot.

The members of the TIO clique were trying hard to stand their ground, but it wasn't looking good for them. The 357 Mobb was advancing on them like a military platoon.

Stacy had almost made it to the building. She was less than ten feet away from it when a stray slug burrowed into her back. The bullet took a chunk of her heart with it as it exploded out of her chest. She was dead before her body hit the ground. Another innocent soul stolen by the predators of the jungle.

Nardy almost tripped over Stacy's fallen body as he and Lil' Dooka rounded the corner of the building, running full speed to help their brothers. Nardy jumped over Stacy. When his feet landed on the ground, he lifted the Draco and let it do its thang. Lil' Dooka did the same with his Glock 17.

The two new shooters brought a new element to the shootout, and Murda knew it. He could make out the sounds of at least eight different guns shooting from the opposite direction. Murda switched his attention to the new shooters and sent some bullets their way. It did little to detour the new shooters.

Finally realizing that they were in a bad position, CJ called for everybody to fall back and get the fuck out of there. Considering there was nothing to hide behind on Cement Hill, it was unbelievable that more bodies didn't drop, but the fun had just started.

Chapter 9

"I'm telling you, homie, that shit was super crazy! Mutha-fuckas damn near stampeded out that muthafucka! Me and the homies just made it out of there without getting caught up in that shit." Smokey was filling Chino in on what went down the other night at Skrew's Better Living concert.

The two were sitting inside of Chino's 1998 Monte Carlo SS. The red, two-door Monte Carlo was Chino's pride and joy. He bought the car for himself as a gift for his 18th birthday. Chino and Smokey were parked a little ways down the street from Issa's store on 21st and Alabama. They were keeping their eyes on the gang's street drug sales operation.

Chino took a bite out of his chicharron pupusa. Hot cheese ran down his chin from the delicious pupusa. "I'm saying, ho-mie, that shit was all over the TV. Mayor Breed was even on the TV talking about the rise in gun violence in the city. Cry-ing that same old sad song. Fucking puta knows it's her people that's fucking the city up in the first place, pinche negrito (fucking niggers)."

Chino secretly hated black people. To him, the fucking niggers were always fucking things up. They didn't think half of the time before they did the stupid shit that they did. The only reason he dealt with Lil' Dooka on any kind of level was because Crazy wouldn't allow any of the homies to sell any kind of drug other than crystal meth. Which was why they got their personal drugs from Lil' Dooka, but if Chino could help it, all of that was going to change.

"Word on the linea (line) is them the same fools that shot up the Fo' the other night. Fools are saying yo' boy Dooka and his TIO niggaz are at war with them 357 cats." Smokey took a bit of his pupusa.

"Who, them fools from Double Rock? I thought them fools were out of the streets?" Chino remembered when a couple of the members of the 357 Mobb were robbing the D-boys on the block.

"Yeah. Those were the fools that shot up the connect. I heard that one of the USOs in Tear It Off disrespected that fool C1ty's old lady. Shit got out of hand and now them fools are at war." Smokey took another bite of his pupusa and reached for his Jarritos to wash it down.

"Who cares? Fuck all them jungle monkeys! I hope they all kill each other off to save us from having to do it." Chino was beginning to get angry just talking about them fucking monkeys.

He then threw the rest of his pupusa back in the bag it came in. He had lost his fucking appetite. A commotion drew his attention back to the front of the store. One of the lil' homies had some fool jacked up against the wall. The lil' homie was yelling and beating the shit out of the dude.

"What the fuck?" Chino was out of the car instantly. Smokey was right behind him. Within seconds, they were both in front of the store in the midst of the homies.

"Pee-Wee! Hey, be smooth, homie, we ain't trynna get the spot hot!" Chino stepped in between Pee-Wee and the fool that he was beating up. "What's up, fool?"

Pee-Wee was breathing heavy from the exertion of beating on the dude. "This bitch ass muthafucka thought he could bring his ass over here wit' some fake ass counterfeit money like it's sweet over here or something."

As if to vouch for what Pee-Wee just said, another one the lil' homies started waving two bills in the air. Chino snatched the bills out of the little muthafucka's hand. He knew the small scene drew some attention from passersby. Chino could feel the eyes on him. He looked at the white boy. One of his eyes had swollen shut by then. Blood leaked from his broken nose and split lip. Chino wanted to do far worse to the muthafucka for his disrespect. The problem was, the guy was white. One look at his expensive, but non-flashy clothes said he came from money. What if he was somebody important or related to somebody important? They didn't need the kind of heat it would draw to the block if they seriously fucked him up.

Chino really didn't understand white people. It was clear as day that dude had money, but instead of just spending that money, he would rather come down to their block with some counterfeit shit. That was the kind of shit white people did.

Chino stepped up as close as he could, getting directly into the white boy's face. "Give me a teener!" He reached his hand out to no one in particular, never taking his eyes off the white boy.

One of the lil' homies immediately responded to the command by placing a sixteenth of an ounce of crystal meth into Chino's open hand. Chino took the teener along with the counterfeit money and shoved it into the frightened white boy's front shirt pocket forcefully.

"Now listen real good, white boy, the only reason you're walking out of here is I'm in a good mood today. But if you bring yo' bitch ass back around here trying to pull some bullshit again, you won't be lucky a second time!"

Even though he could only see thru one eye, and the vision in that one eye was somewhat blurry, the white boy could see the danger inside of Chino's eyes.

"You hear me, bitch?" Spittle flew from Chino's mouth into the white boy's face.

Frightened out of his mind, the white boy franticly nodded his head up and down. He understood. He thought to himself that he should've went down to the Tenderloins like he usually did. The dope wasn't as good as up here, but he never had a problem passing off money down there. The hustlers were a lot dumber down in the Tenderloin District.

"Now get the fuck outta my hood, bitch!" Chino roughly shoved the white boy. He kicked him in the ass like the bitch he was. The white boy stumbled after getting kicked in the ass by Chino. He didn't care though. He was the type of person to always try to find the good in everything. And as he touched his swollen eye, he thought to himself that they could have done a lot more to him than they did. He finally made it to his Audi A-8. Driving off, he thought of the second good thing. He had gotten the dope and still had his money. With that in mind, he decided to head over to the Tenderloins. He couldn't see any good reason why he shouldn't go get more dope since he still had the money.

After barking out orders to make sure things went back to normal on the block, Chino left Smokey in charge of the block. He himself had a meeting that he wasn't going to miss or be late for. This meeting was crucial to the plans that Chino had for the future. The plans he had for the new familia. He wouldn't miss this meeting for the world. Chino climbed back into his Monte Carlo. Before he left, he pulled his phone out and searched for "El Negro" in his contacts. All he typed was four words in the text message box once he pulled it up.

"I'm on my way." He pressed send, then pulled off with blood and money on his mind.

***

C1ty sat hunched over in his wheelchair on the side of G-Baby's hospital bed. Openly, he cried. He cried at the pain he felt in his heart from the sight of his only love laid out before his eyes in a coma. He cried out of shame. The shame of knowing that G-Baby was fighting for her life because he failed to do his job. He failed to protect her!

Four bullets violated her body during the shootout. The first two entered her abdomen. One exited out her back while the second one pierced her large intestine. The last bullet tore through her upper chest. Yet it was the third bullet that caused the most harm to her body. It entered her chest cavity, nicking one of her arteries as it passed by. As fate would have it, the bullet then ricocheted off the back of her rib cage and came back out of the front of her chest. It pierced her lung in the process.

The paramedics lost G-Baby once in the ambulance on the ride to the hospital. That wasn't all, the doctors had to revive her twice more on the operating table. It took the team of surgeons twenty-three hours to repair what they could of the damage the bullets did to her young body. Now it was up to Genesis herself to fight for recovery.

Through water-blurred eyes, C1ty stared at his beloved. All the wires and tubes connected to machines that were attached to her body, made her look uncomfortable to him. The nurses assured C1ty that G-Baby didn't feel any discomfort from the vast amount of tubes and wires. Their assurances did little to ease his mind.

Initially, Genesis' father wouldn't allow C1ty to see his daughter, blaming C1ty for her being shot to begin with. It was her mother who finally convinced her father that what happened to their daughter could happen to anyone. Especially after the police report stated that C1ty came to their daughter's aide and defense in the club, which was what led to the shooting.

His own personal wounds and pain were meaningless to him as he sat and cried over his baby. There was no doubt that he was about to be on a mad hunt for that nigga named revenge. He and C1ty had a date of their own.

CJ had been by the hospital earlier to check on C1ty and give him a report about the shit they did in Sunnydale the other night. It wasn't enough in C1ty's eyes. Not with G-Baby laying up in a fucking hospital bed looking like some fucking science experiment. He wanted the streets to flow with a river of blood. He had no way of knowing just how true that wish was about to become.

"Everything's ready, brah." Wes didn't want to bother his little brother, but it was time for them to go.

Never in all their live could Wes ever recall seeing so much hurt and pain on his little brother's face. The burden of pain wasn't C1ty's to carry alone. Wes loved G-Baby too.

75

They all did. She was the perfect complement for C1ty. Before the two of them hooked up, C1ty was the wildest out of the entire bunch. His gunplay was unmatched, and his temper second to none. Like the seasons, his recklessness changed the moment G-Baby came into his life. It was her love that tamed the wild beast that was inside of him. Unfortunately, that beast was just dumped out of its cage and the Beast Master was in a coma, unable to control it.

"Let's go then." C1ty didn't want to leave, but he had to. Sitting there doing nothing but crying would kill him.

Wes walked up behind the wheelchair and wheeled his little brother out of the hospital room and down the hallways. About halfway down the second hallway, C1ty made Wes stop. Nothing about his injuries prevented C1ty from walking. He was in the wheelchair solely due to hospital policy. However, he wasn't about to let his men see him in a fucking wheelchair! No sign of weakness would be displayed by C1ty. Therefore, he said fuck the hospital and its policy. He stood up slowly and marched out of the hospital in pain, but with his back straight and head held high.

The young general was about to lead his troops into battle. C1ty was about to wage war.

Chapter 10

The constant ringing of his cell phone was nagging at Monster, fucking up his concentration. Irritated, he snatched his cell phone out of his pocket. It took some maneuvering, but he finally managed. A picture of his old lady, Lupe, was on the screen.

Monster loved Lupe with all his heart. She was 8 ½ months pregnant with their second baby, which meant she was stingy with the pussy. She hadn't given Monster any ass going on three months now. Love didn't have shit to do with a nutt, especially to a 25-year-old nigga. He pressed ignore on the phone. He may have loved Lupe, but he wasn't about to let her fuck up his nutt. The little snow bunny that was sucking his dick was so vicious with her head game that he was ready to bust his nutt any minute. The little bitch was using so much spit that it was literally running down his balls into the crack of his ass.

He didn't even bother trying to put the phone back inside his pocket. He just let it drop to the floor. He looked down at the snow bunny with the Harley Quinn dyed hair. She was sucking his dick like she was trying to win the Olympic dick suck'n contest.

Monster knew he couldn't hold back too much longer, not the way this bitch was performing. He laid his head back on the headrest and closed his eyes, ready to greet his climax. He never saw the shadowy figure that walked up to his driver side window holding a gun, nor the bullet that it sent crashing into his skull, killing him instantly. The fucked-up part about it all was Monster never even felt the climax as his balls released the semen that was built up in them.

The snow bunny never flinched nor screamed. The timing was perfect. She didn't know if her accomplice would get there in time to prevent her from having to swallow a mouthful of nutt. Having to suck the sweaty Mexican's small dick was bad enough, she didn't want to have to swallow his nutt too. Luckily for her, she didn't have to. She quickly looked in the mirror, making sure there was no blood on her, and adjusted herself, making sure she was appropriate before exiting the truck.

By the time she was out of the truck, the shadowy figure had already walked back to the waiting getaway vehicle. She casually walked over to him, got in the car, and popped a stick of Winterfresh gum into her mouth while her accomplice drove off into the night.

***

Chino pulled up to the big estate and parked. Even in the dark of night the house looked massive. The estate's high walls ensured privacy from neighbors. The front lawn was huge itself. The Monte Carlo headlights revealed that the lawn was also freshly manicured. After being buzzed in the front security gate, he drove up to the front of the house.

Earlier in the day, when Chino sent El Negro the text message informing him that he was on his way, El Negro had called Chino and told him they had to reschedule due to a pressing matter that came up. Initially Chino was pissed, but there wasn't much he could do. The truth was Chino needed El Negro. As long as the big homies were against selling any other drugs except meth, Chino couldn't use any of their connects as a pipeline to feed him the drugs that he wanted.

Chino figured he would take the initiative to show the big homies that change was good for the family. He would get the supply that he needed from El Negro to be able to start doing his thang. Once he was established enough to step to the big homies, they would see the potential benefits to the organization of selling the other drugs. Chino knew the big homies would not only agree to changing the old policy, but he also believed they would give him the rank that he so desired by making him a general.

By the time he made it out of the car and to the front door, it was already opened. He was greeted, let in the house, and led into one of the studies by a pretty African American girl about Chino's age. He knew he was out of pocket for watching the way her hips swayed and her ass bounced as she walked. It didn't stop him, though. Being from Frisco, Chino saw plenty of chicks with a nice phat ass. But something was different about hers. In a sense, it was perfect.

When they entered the study, Egypt turned around in time to catch Chino staring openly at her ass. He just knew she was about to flip out on him. He was shocked when she looked him up and down and smiled. "You're not ready, Lil' Daddy. Have a seat and Rick will be in here shortly." With the same smile on her face, she turned to walk out of the study. Before doing so, she looked over her right shoulder and jokingly told Chino, "Enjoy."

Chino was dumbfounded. Her behavior and comment was the last thing he had expected from the 5'4" butter pecan complexion beauty. With a smile on his face to match hers, he took her advice and enjoyed the view. It was a good one. It was so good, in fact, that he was still staring seconds after she had already turned the corner. Taking a seat on the leather couch inside of the study, Chino decided he was going to have to get to know the little cutie on an intimate level.

Egypt walked down the hallway still smiling as she thought about the bold Mexican gangbanger that openly stared at her ass like it was a juicy, mouthwatering watermelon. Egypt loved the excitement of living on the edge, which was why she was her uncle's favorite niece. She was what most people called a sweet poison, because of her beautiful looks. Mostly every man would mistakenly overlook the warning signs their minds gave them when they looked at her. Blinded by their lust, most men would never see her deadly traits until it was too late. It was her appetite for excitement that had her entertaining the idea of toying with the little Mexican just to see how bold he really was.

Egypt nearly ran into her uncle as she rounded the corner of the hallway. "Ooh! Excuse me, Uncle." She stopped abruptly just before bumping into him.

Out of pure reflective instincts, Rick reached out both of his hands, catching her just above her elbows to help balance her. "It's okay, baby, are you okay?"

"Yes, I'm fine. Your guest is in your study waiting for you. Do you need me for anything else?" she asked her uncle as she stepped out of his embrace.

"No, Egypt, I got everything from here, hon. Thanks," Rick told his niece before walking off down the hallway.

Rick entered the study and closed the door behind him for privacy. He noticed Chino seated on one of the two leather sofas.

"I'm glad my schedule change didn't keep you from making it," Rick told Chino as Chino stood and the two men shook hands.

"It would've taken more than a little juggling of time to prevent something this big from happening," Chino told him.

"Glad to hear what's priority to you. Would you care for anything to drink?" Rick made his way over to the bar.

"Naaw, I'm good, big homie." Chino sat back down on the sofa.

Rick fixed himself a glass of Hennessy, then he walked over to the second sofa and took a seat. The house was old Georgian style. The rooms were all massive including the study. The furniture was a mix of old ancient style wood with old English leather. A person could tell that Rick came from money. His natural presence dripped authority. The interior feeling of the study did wonders enhancing Rick's aura of authority.

"Chino, let's get straight down to it. Your proposal is more than enticing. I took a little time doing some research and calculating my own projected figures, and I believe your numbers, although very impressive, are actually very modest. By my calculations, if you take care of everything that you need to take care of in order for us to proceed with plans, then I believe we should be able to do triple the numbers you predict." Rick took a moment to sip from his glass. "With numbers that impressive, I'm willing to stand behind you one hundred percent. In fact, I'm actually willing to lend you a hand in getting your affairs in order."

Chino was hoping that El Negro would agree to his proposal. However, he wasn't expecting for it to be so easy. He was expecting to have to convince the old man first. Hearing that El Negro was also willing to help make the transition a lot easier was another plus. Chino knew as well as anyone that Rick was a powerful man. With his help and him standing behind Chino once he took over as the head of 21st, no one would be able to stop him or his army from branching out further than just the Mission District.

"Big homie, I guarantee you that I'll handle my end of everything. I've never been a man that couldn't handle my own business. At the same time, I'm not no dummy either. Having your support and help could only speed things up for me, which would be better for the both of us. So, if you're offering some assistance, then I'm not turning it down."

"I figured you'd say that, so I took the initiative to send one of my associates out to visit one of our little friends already. I figured that would get the ball running. As soon as you get all your loose ends tied up, we should be ready to proceed. At that time, we can go over and finalize all the numbers." Rick took another swallow of the smooth brown liquid.

Chino wondered what El Negro was telling him. He was going to ask him but thought better of it. Shit, whatever he was talking about would be known sooner or later. Chino's mind was on all the money he was about to make and the power that came along with it. He knew the numbers he gave El Negro were slightly low. He was trying to see where the old man's head was. By Chino's calculations, 21st Street alone should be able to sell a kilo of coke every week. Maybe every three days, if he and his soldiers could take over the whole Mission. Granted, a lot of palms would have to be greased. Even still, at the end of the day, Chino would be El Jefe (The Boss), and he was about to get paid.

"I'll get to cleaning up my front yard immediately, big homie. It shouldn't take me no time to get into position. I'm thinking I'll be ready for the first shipment at the end of two weeks." Chino's greed drove his confidence through the roof. He couldn't wait for the day to come when he bought himself a house like this one. Because he knew the day would come.

He would make sure that day came!

Chapter 11

It was already seventy something degrees outside on a clear sunny morning. A gentle breeze blew, carrying the sounds of the hood on its wings. The sound of cries and screams could be heard over church music that drifted along the gentle breeze as well.

Through his tear-stained eyes, the sunlight played games with young Mari's vision. The seventeen-year-old was the youngest member of TIO. He was also the younger brother of Turk. Mari and Turk were close but not as close as Mari had been to Bubz. The two of them had more of a brother-brother relationship than Mari and Turk did.

The pain was evident on young Mari. Though he sat parked out in front of River of Life, the church on Sunnydale Avenue, he couldn't bring himself to exit the four-door black Beamer (BMW) and walk into the church. His pain was too great, his heart too heavy. After smoking three blunts since being parked there, the weed smoke was so thick the inside of the BMW looked like it was on fire. Mari paid the smoke no attention. As he lifted the fourth blunt, which he'd just lit, to his lips, his entire physical body was numb, but nothing eased the emotional pain. The words of the song said it all!

"I wish I knew when the storm came (storm came)/How many tears did you cry when you lost someone?/We did this shit all for the gutter, whoa, whoa, whoa/Did this shit for my lil' brother, whoa (brother), whoa, whoa/Had to stand through these tears 'cause I see you every time my eyes close/Asking myself why you had to go, but only God knows (only God knows)."

The tears rained down. Mari couldn't understand it. Fuck God had to take his dawg for? Of all the fuck niggaz in the world, why his muthafuck'n dawg? It felt like Roddy Ricch understood all of his pain. He couldn't let anyone see his hurt, but through his tinted windows, Mari let the pain wash down his face.

The front doors of the church opened. People began to file out slowly, lining up on either side of the walkway. They were making an aisle outside of the church that the pallbearers could walk down as they carried the casket. Mari sat the lit blunt down in the ashtray. He had to get outside of the car and stand next to his brothers. He used the bottom of his shirt to wipe the tears from his face. No matter how many times he tried to gather his composure and wipe his face, fresh tears would take the place of the ones just removed.

A few of the people who were unable to hold their composure decided to walk to their cars. Once the church let out, everyone was headed to the Colma Cemetery to pay their last respects as Bubz was laid to rest. As the casket came into view, Nardy and Lil' Dooka were the first two pallbearers. Creep-Thru and Turk were behind Nardy, and T.G. and Reco were behind Lil' Dooka. Waka, A-Wax, and MoMo were walking in front of Bubz's mom, who was going hysterical, and the rest of the family. They were about five or so feet behind the casket.

Suddenly, Bubz's mom broke free from A-Wax, who was holding her. She ran screaming and crying, "I want my baby! Give me back my baby!" to the front of Lil' Dooka and Nardy, making the procession stand still. She slapped Lil' Dooka hard across the face. The slap was hard and loud. Still frantic, she began punching Lil' Dooka all over while screaming, "Give me my son! Give me back my fucking son!"

Bubz's mom's antics were so outrageous that they drew the attention of everybody outside. No one saw the two Jeep Cherokees as they pulled up and stopped in the middle of the street. The Jeep in front was white. The second one was a charcoal grey. Both had tinted windows, which all rolled down at the same time, in sync.

The loud sounds of automatic gunfire instantly snatched everyone's attention away from the sounds of Bubz's mom's screams as they were drowned out by the gunfire. Bubz's mom was the first casualty. So many bullets crashed into her body, jerking her wildly, like she was under attack by a swarm of angry hornets.

The last thing A-Wax intended to do before a .223 knocked a chunk of his skull off was to get to Bubz's mom before she made Lil' Dooka drop her son's casket. Unfortunately, intentions weren't actions. Even if he had made it to Momma Bubz in time, it would not have made a difference. The bullets that riddled Creep-Thru's chest made sure of that! Not only did Creep-Thru let go of the casket, but the force of the bullets hitting his body knocked him into Turk, who lost his balance, forcing him to let go of his hold on the casket as well.

Like a house made of cards blown by the wind, the casket carrying Bubz's body tumbled over, spilling the dead TIO member out onto the fallen bodies of Turk and Creep-Thru.

MoMo was the first to respond. He snatched twin Glock .23s off the front of his waist and began busting back. 4-Boy and Waka joined MoMo and sent hot shit toward the two Jeeps. Bullet holes appeared like magic on the side of both Jeeps. The far back window of the white Jeep shattered into a thousand little black pieces.

Lil' Dooka's first instincts were to help Mama Bubz. One look at her limp body on the ground told him there wasn't shit he could do for her. Instead, he took aim at the driver's side window of the first Jeep. Unfortunately, his timing was off. At that moment, the white Jeep's driver punched down on the gas, and the vehicle surged forward in response. The second Jeep followed in pursuit. The drivers of the Jeeps were so focused on speeding away that neither of them saw the tall, chubby Asian with the curly afro emerge from the black BMW that was parked a little ways down the street, with the AK-47 in his hands.

When Mari squeezed the trigger, the loud, thunderous roar of the AK-47 shook most of the funeral attendees to the core. It was an unmistakable sound to those familiar with it. Mari did his best to try to contain the beast in his hands, but his best attempt was useless. When he brought the assault rifle to life, Mari wasn't ready for its fierce, raw power. The heavy gun got away from him, sending its mini missiles flying all over the place. It was purely luck that the beginning of the barrage of bullets hit their target. They ate up the front of the white Jeep like it was candy and the bullets had a sweet tooth.

Behind the tinted windows of the white Jeep, CJ made the mistake of attempting to swerve out of the way of the choppa's spray while the Jeep was powerfully accelerating. The mistake was made because Mari's sudden gun burst caught CJ by surprise, causing him to panic. Realizing his mistake, CJ yanked the steering wheel in the opposite direction. The Jeep responded, but the damage was already done.

The front passenger side of the Jeep crashed into a red Toyota Camry that was parked on the street. Wes was in the passenger seat of the white Jeep. His head smacked into the windshield with so much force that it not only split his forehead, making him dizzy, but it also cracked the windshield.

C1ty didn't panic. He swerved to the left and hit the gas pedal. The charcoal-colored Jeep lurched forward, barreling down on Mari. He saw the second Jeep coming toward him at a high speed. Mari wanted to swing the choppa around and eat it up, but he couldn't gain control of it.

Lil' Dooka saw what C1ty was trying to do. He wasn't about to let that shit happen! Lil' Dooka sent shot after shot at the Jeep. It didn't detour C1ty. People were driving all over the place and running everywhere in hopes of dodging all the stray bullets that were soaring through the air. Mari jumped out of the way just in time to avoid getting ran over. C1ty adjusted the wheel while hitting the brakes. This positioned him so that he was blocking the drivers' side of the white Jeep from the relentless hail of bullets coming from the church's direction.

CJ turned the key in the ignition, praying that the Jeep would restart, but nothing happened. Murda wasn't going to be a sitting fucking duck. He opened the back driver's side door and hopped out firing. His first bullet flew an inch past MoMo's head, landing in the door jam. This caused MoMo to drop down to one knee. He continued to shoot and return fire.

Murda continued to squeeze. He didn't give two fucks about the bullets flying past his head. Just as Murda sent two slugs intended for MoMo's head, some stupid fuck chose that moment to try to dart away, crossing in front of MoMo. Two slugs tore through the stupid muthafucka's stomach.

This time, the Jeep started when CJ turned the key. He hit the horn signaling to Murda it was time to go. Murda sent a few more shots in the direction of the church. He was pissed that the stupid fuck had gotten in his way. He jumped back in the Jeep, and both vehicles sped off. They raced down Sunnydale like two angry, demonic Autobots fleeing from the Decepticons.

The carnage that was left behind at the church was unbelievable. Bodies of the wounded were all over the place. The causalities would later be determined to be seven dead and another fourteen wounded. Both A-Wax and Creep-Thru were counted with the dead.

This was only the beginning!

Chapter 12

Lil' Dooka couldn't believe what he was seeing as he looked around. The front of the church looked like a military battle-field. The dead were littered among the wounded. Helplessly, the wounded cried out for assistance. The sulfuric smell of gun powder or gun smoke was thick enough to choke some of the people in the area. Faint wisps of smoke still drifted off the tip of the empty gun he carried on his hip.

He could hear the sirens of the police and emergency re-sponse crews that were responding to calls of the shootout that had just taken place.

There were so many things that Lil' Dooka wanted to do. Help the wounded, see about Bubz's mom, right the toppled over, bullet-riddled casket, help put Bubz's lifeless body back inside of the casket. So much more. However, the approaching sirens, the bodies strewn about the street, and the gun in his hand told him that he needed to get himself and his brothers out of the area.

He did just that.

Knowing that they wouldn't be any good to anybody if they were all locked down at the county jail on 850 Bryant was all the motivation and or convincing any of his brothers needed to listen to his advice and get the fuck out of there.

***
(a couple of hours later)

MoMo, Turk, 4-Boy, Reco, Waka, Nardy, and T.G. all sat crammed inside of the tiny room inside Nardy and Lil' Dooka's auntie's apartment. The block was hot as fuck! It seemed like half the district's police force responded to the shootout. It was on every Bay Area news station and all the major stations throughout the rest of California. The fellas all caught the news when they first came to the spot. Everybody wanted to see what was the word being reported. They all needed to see if anybody went against the code of the streets and talked to the police. Once they were all satisfied that they heard all that they were going to hear, the news became obsolete.

The room door opened. Mari came back into the room from using the bathroom. He walked in and found a spot on the floor. He looked around at all the faces in the room. Everybody was lost in their own world. Mari couldn't take it. The silence was fucking with him.

"It seem like everybody lost somewhere else right now. I know niggaz got a lot of shit on they minds right about now, but we need to be talking about what the fuck we about to do." Mari was embarrassed about the fact that he let the choppa get away from him, but he was still a ridah.

"Fuck you think we gone do? We gone slide on dem bitch ass niggaz," Turk spat. Sometimes he hated the dumb shit his little brother said.

"Nigga, I know we gone slide, but we gotta figure out exactly how we gone do it. In case you ain't checked the fucking score board, nigga, we losing dis bitch. And them bitch ass niggaz ain't just normal niggaz. They money already up! How in the fuck you think we about to war with niggaz chipped up and we broke as fuck?" Mari would swear to God his brother was the stupidest muthafucka he had ever met.

"Nigga, fuck money! All I need is my gun and my bullets and I'm ready fo' whatever," Waka threw in his two cents.

"And how yo' stupid ass supposed to buy them bullets you using? And I guess you gonna keep using the same gun to continue bussing drills, bitch?" Mari thought Waka's wannabe ass was just as dumb as Turk.

"Lil' nigga's right. I don't care how you look at it. Everybody know you don't go to war if yo' bag ain't up. We fa'sho in the middle of a war, so we need to do something. That goes without saying. But we need a bag, too, 'cause wars cost money," 4-Boy broke his silence.

"All that philosophy and strategy shit sounds cool and all, but right now we need to body some shit. 'Cause muthafuckas was mad disrespectful!" Reco was mad as fuck! "Niggaz ain't 'bout to be round here thinking shit sweet!"

"Bodying something right now ain't gone solve our problem. 4-Boy and Mari right. We need to come up with a plan for after we bust our doll. 'Cause it's time to turn da fuck up!" MoMo rolled a blunt as he was talking. He needed to calm his nerves. He was already on edge. Talking wasn't doing shit but pissing him off more.

"It ain't even a question, we fa'sho finna ride, nigga, that's on BR Ain't no way in hell we gone let this ride. Boy, I hear you. We gotta plan for the bigger picture, and on BR, brah, we gone do that. But I'll be damned if another sun rise without one of them bitches in the ground—" Lil' Dooka began, but 4-Boy cut him off.

"Dooka, nigga, how we supposed to ride out tonight with the block on fire like it is?" 4-Boy looked at Lil' Dooka like he'd lost his mind.

"You sound stupid, 4-Boy! Nigga, I don't give a fuck 'bout da police, and that's on BR, nigga!" Lil' Dooka spat, starting to get pissed off at 4-Boy. "Nigga, did you not just see how they did Bubz's moms? Nigga, if that was yo' mama, you'd want niggaz to ride out too!"

"Naaw, Dook, Boy got a good point. Nigga, we gone ride on them niggaz, that's on BR, cuz. But we gotta be smooth. Losing niggaz to this street shit is one thing, but getting caught up 'cause we ain't moving right is another. That ain't 'bout shit, and it ain't gone do shit but sit niggaz on they pockets down at 850 looking real sick while them bitch niggaz still out here looking and living good!" Reco was ready to rock and roll just like the rest of his brothers. He wasn't trying to get caught up on no stupid shit and be gone hella long. Shit, June went down back in 2013 and he still fighting his shit!

Lil' Dooka wasn't trying to hear none of that listen to reason shit. Deep down, though, he knew his brothers were right. Deep down, he knew he had to put his fucking feelings in his pockets. It was time to man up or man down, and he'd die before he went man down.

"Man fuck! Blood! I ain't trynna lose no more of you niggaz, and that's on BR I know you niggaz right, though, this muthafucka is on fire. That's cool, though, it just means it's time to Tear It Off! Since we need our bands up to go to war, we about to get our bands up. But, bitch, on BR, the bread we 'bout to get gone all go toward taking them bitch ass Double Rock niggaz to war! I don't care if they 357 or not! If a nigga from Double Rock, he gone get it. I hope you niggaz been putting money away like Budda told you niggaz to. 'Cause that's the money niggaz gone have to live off of for a minute. Don't get me wrong, niggaz gone be able to take home some of the chips from these next licks. But the majority of shit gone go in the kitty. I'mma holla at the homie and get some shit lined up. We gone fall back on that other shit till it's time. But I swear to God, on BR, nigga, when it's time, we gone have us a real nigga holiday!"

"Yeah, bitch. That's on BR" Nardy knew the look he saw on his cousin's face. That playboy shit was a wrap. They was about to be on that demon shit.

BR was Baby Reno. He was the very first casualty the TIO clique ever suffered. They lived this shit and would die in this shit all for his name!

Chapter 13

"I am glad to see that you are well. Being that I didn't originally know the extent of your injuries when I heard the news, I was wondering if I would see your young face again." The old man leaned over and dumped the ashes from his Grand Daddy Purple Kush-filled blunt into the ashtray that sat on the marble and glass table.

"Shit, brah, I'm not even 'bout to try and sound gangsta and tell you I wasn't fazed by that shit. But on some real shit, brah, when that shit popped off and I saw them first shots hit my baby, all caution and self-preservation went right out the window. The only thing that mattered to me was G-Baby. Protecting her was of the utmost, because my life couldn't continue to exist without her." C1ty's voice trailed off. He didn't even dare to entertain the notion of him never being able to hold, kiss, or make love to G-Baby ever again.

Spank-G knew exactly how C1ty felt. He himself had once been a wild, dope-selling, street-running, gang-busting beast. He was originally born in Chicago, Illinois. He moved to California at the age of 10 and landed in San Francisco's Sunnydale Projects. At 11, he started stealing cars with some friends. By age 12, he bought his first gun, a 38 Special, which he needed to protect his newfound investment: selling drugs.

Spank-G's clique was small, but they were mean. A team of wolves made up of Marcell, Dada-D, Pops, Cory, O-Jay, and himself. The six of them terrorized the turfs of San Francisco from Double Rock to Filmore.

Spank-G caught his first body at 13, and they quickly began to pile up as his name spread like a California wildfire through the streets of San Francisco. His gun-blazing, toe-tagging ways eventually caught up with him, and he ended up serving almost 15 years for a body. It was toward the end of his sentence that he met and fell in love with Trina of the She-Wolves. They started their relationship off slowly, but it grew strong and fast at its own rapid pace. Now, years later, Spank-G couldn't begin to imagine living life without his Queen by his side.

"I understand what you mean, young ridah, which is why I understand that play you just put down. But I remind you, as much as it may hurt us to do so, we can't allow our emotions to cloud our judgement nor get in the way of our true objective. If so, we run the risk of losing it all."

C1ty caught the subliminal about the play he just put down as a reference to the shooting at Cement Hill and the shooting of the church the other day. He didn't feel the need to comment on it. What was done was done. However, he knew Spank-G's other inuendo was in regard to their business.

"I assure you, brah, I'm not about to let nothing get in the way of business or our goal. This little shit wasn't nothing but a few kids needing to be taught the ramifications of playing kid games with grown ass men." C1ty searched for the MCM backpack that rested on the ground between them and handed it to Spank-G. "Here is your usual from the last job. The next one is lined up on track and on schedule like we planned."

Spank-G ashed his blunt again before grabbing the bag. They were out by the pool in his backyard. Spank-G liked young C1ty. He was smart, honest, and loyal. All of which were good traits to look for in someone you were doing business with. There was no need to look inside of the bag. He knew every dollar would be accounted for. Spank-G didn't want to disrespect C1ty by looking into the bag down on the ground. Next, he searched for his glass of Hennessey and took a good swallow.

"If all goes well and you guys continue to handle yourselves in a professional manner, all of you will have enough money to do whatever you want in life. Have you given any thought to what you want to do?"

C1ty reached for his own glass of Hennessey. "Honestly, brah, I do this shit to ensure I'm able to give Genesis everything she could ever want. As far as setting a future goes, my

94

future is whatever she wants. As long as she is by my side, that's all that matters to me, brah."

His comment made him think about G-Baby laying up in the hospital fighting for her life. This made him want to go back over to Sunnydale and knock some more shit down.

Spank-G saw the pain on young C1ty's face. It was written clear as day over all of his features. C1ty didn't say it. He didn't have to. The look on his face told Spank-G that they were about to have a real serious problem.

***

(Hillsborough, California)

The PG&E truck pulled to a stop in front of the house. Moments later, a PG&E van pulled alongside of the truck. The two drivers held a very brief conversation, then the van backed into the driveway that ran along the side of the house. The driver of the truck climbed out and made his way to the front door.

It was little after 10:00 in the morning. Most everyone on this street and in this neighborhood was up and busy with their day. To any of the remaining neighbors at home, it wasn't out of the ordinary to see PG&E crews working on the roads or on certain properties in the area. The homes, like the power lines in the area, were old and required constant repair and upkeep.

The driver of the truck knocked on the front door of the big house and rang the doorbell for a full five minutes. Accepting that no one was home, he walked to the side of the house to find the utility box. Once there, he inconspicuously glanced around before removing a two-way walkie talkie from his pocket. He never said a word. He simply clicked the talk button twice and placed the walkie talkie back inside of his pocket.

Seconds later, the back of the van opened. T.G., 4-Boy, and Turk all climbed out of the van, all dressed like utility workers in knock off PG&E clothes. The three of them followed Waka, who'd left the utility box and walked to the back of the house. The TIO clique was as close to professional burglars as hood niggaz could get. They all started off bipping, which was breaking into parked cars. It was low risk, low time, and very profitable. Hell, they were considered ballers in high school.

The real money came when the big homie, who had been hearing good things about the crew, reached out to Lil' Dooka and made him a deal too good to refuse. The big homie had a network of inside connects, who fed him all the information he needed on houses throughout the Bay Area that were loaded with money and goods for the taking. The big homie would then provide Lil' Dooka with the information for a fee. The fee differed depending on what was supposedly inside the house.

This had been the clique's main source of income ever since. Of course, each member of the clique did their own thing on the side. Shit, everybody was chasing the bag. Right now, though, it was all about stacking their chips in preparation for war.

Waka was the truck driver. Since he was the only white boy in the clique, it only made since for him to be the guy in the uniform that people saw walking up to the front door. That way they wouldn't grow suspicious. Suspicious people never tended to mind their own business. They were too busy being all up in yours.

Once Waka gained entry to the house, he disabled the alarm in less than two minutes. Right away, the Tear It Off Clique came to life. Any and every electronic of value from smart phones to 80-inch flat screen TVs vanished from the residence. Designer bags, jewelry, game consoles, expensive throw rugs, all items of value in a sense became animated and did disappearing acts.

It was also Waka's sole job to locate the main item or items of interests. In this case, there was supposed to be a small safe inside of the walk-in closet in the master bedroom. Waka didn't waste any time finding the safe. The moment he walked in the closet, he thought, *This shit is too easy.*

Not only was the safe right where it was supposed to be, the door was already cracked open. Waka smiled to himself and went to work. In seconds, the safe was empty. He rose to leave when something in the far side of the corner caught his attention. There was a second smaller safe in the corner. The door wasn't open, but Waka wasn't about to leave without trying his luck.

He ran over and crouched down in front of the safe. It was one of the safes you got at Costco for sixty-something dollars. It never had a chance fucking with Waka and his trusted tools. When he opened the door, he paused. He had never in all of his young years seen a prettier sight.

The safe contained nothing but pure gold. Not no bullshit like gold jewelry, but real actual gold. There were these containers inside of the safe that had rows upon rows of some kind of gold coins. He broke out of his hesitant trance and began grabbing the containers. They were a little heavier than he expected but not too heavy. After hitting both safes, he was ready to go. The closet was filled with all kinds of designer purses and bags. Waka used one of the Fendi bags that he saw to load the coins.

As he was coming out of the closet, he literally ran into T.G.

"Bitch, what's taking you so long?" T.G. asked him, not giving a fuck about almost knocking him over.

"Bitch, you ain't going to believe this shit. Come on, grab some of them bags in that bitch and let's get the fuck up out of here!" Waka was juiced. He didn't know what the coins were. All he knew was they were gold. He felt like a real pirate who just found a treasure, or like a real pirate would say: "found some booty!"

T.G. pushed past Waka into the closet and snatched up all the bags, filling up two black garbage bags with them, then he was out.

The nosey neighbor across the street found it pretty peculiar that the PG&E crew was pulling off only 15 or 20 minutes after they pulled up. She figured maybe they found that whatever they came to work on didn't need fixing after all. Later that night, when she learned the reason was because the house had been burglarized that morning, the wife of the owner of one of the largest computer companies in the world was too embarrassed to mention the PG&E crew that she watched at the house earlier that day. After all, she didn't want her neighbors to know how often she spied on them.

Chapter 14

"I'm telling you, homie. They say that the fool had his pants down and his dick out of his boxers. That means, fool, he was either getting some panocha (pussy) or some cabeza (head). Which means he was with a bitch. If it wasn't a set-up, tell me why wasn't a puta (bitch) killed with the homie? And where dat bitch at now?" Trucho was furious that no one was listening to him. He knew what he was saying made pure sense.

The homies were all chilling at Del Sol Park on 25th and Potrero. They were smoking and drinking in honor of Monster, whose body was found in his truck a week ago by a meter maid. The homies were celebrating Monster's life as a way to honor his life instead of mourning it. Too many homies done lost their lives in the name of La Familia (The Family) for them to mourn. For The 21st Crew, dying in the name of La Familia was an honor.

"No one's saying you're wrong, homie. Right now, we got a lot of beef with a lot of cats. What the homies are telling you is that we can't go chasing conspiracy theories. Any one of these fools would love for us to slip just to make them feel confident enough to try to come at us," Tyson, another one of a long list of soldados (soldiers), spoke up.

"Man, fuck dem fools, homie! Dis 21st Street Hogg Status. Fuck the rest!" Little Wero called out, sounding even more drunk than he looked.

"You got that shit right! Fuck them other cats! Army St., 16th, BPL, Natomas. Fool, any one of them muthafuckas can get it if they want it!" Smokey added.

"You got that shit right! Fuck all of them fools! But Trucho's got a point that we can't afford to overlook." Chino saw the shock in his younger brother's face, but he ignored him. "We gotta keep our eyes and our ears open, homies, because it's for too easy to overlook the treachery or miss one of the snakes in the grass until that muthafucka bites you. Then it's too late!"

"Especially if that muthafucka is veno (poisonous)!" At the sound of the voice that spoke, most of the soldados tensed up.

Chino turned to greet the man who spoke. "What's up, big homie?"

"Chino, what's up, lil' homie." Blinky returned Chino's greeting while giving the young soldier the one-arm gangsta hug.

Fanso a.k.a. "Blinky" was 6'2", 200 pounds of pure solid muscle. Calling Blinky a natural born beast and killer would be a severe understatement. When pushed, Blinky was pure evil. Hell, the Devil wouldn't want to fuck with Blinky on a good day. He was Crazy's right-hand man and second in command of the 21st. He had many tattoos on his muscular body, but it was the Hogg Status that was spelled down both arms that told people what he represented and lived for.

"Shit, just trying to celebrate the homie the way he should be celebrated. While at the same time, mentally trying to figure this shit out." Chino took a sip out of the bottle of Corona that he had in his hand.

"Sounded like you fools were doing more than mental figuring when I walked up. That's cool, though, because the big homies have been discussing this shit too. They feel like it could possibly be more to Monster's death than what it appears! He had some Skante (meth) that the big Homie Hector had asked Crazy if he could assist him getting to his nephew, Fat Boy, from MMN. Crazy said yeah and gave the responsibility to Monster. The policía (police) found the drugs inside of Monster's truck when they found his body. That rules out a robbery or a come up!" Blinky knew something more was at play. He could feel it in his gut. He just didn't know what.

"How much dope was it?" Wero stupidly asked.

"Don't matter how much it was, the big Homie Hector asking of it as a favor tells you it was a lot. The fact that it wasn't taken says even more," Chino responded instead of Blinky. He couldn't believe Wero would ask such a stupid question.

Not only could Chino feel what Blinky wasn't saying, he fully understood the implied ramifications of what this could cause. Hector was the big homie over The Natomas, their neighboring brothers. Potentially, if this wasn't handled correctly, this one murder could set the two largest and most powerful Norteno Gangs in all of San Francisco against each other and start a war. This would present a major problem, because Norte laws specifically stated that there was to be no red on red at any time, which meant they weren't supposed to attack or fight one another. Of course, that shit still happened, and the consequences were real severe.

Blinky nodded his head up and down at Chino's comment. The big homies had been paying attention to the lil' soldado. His heart, love for the family, and his thinking ability told them all that he was maturing and growing into a well-respected homie. If he kept up the way he was going, he was sure to become an N-Sol and maybe even a big homie one day.

"Chino, you're always on point. All of the homies see that. The lil' homies love and respect you, and the big homies have started to notice you. That's why I came over here. The homies decided that it's time for you to step up." Some of the younger homies grew excited. A little murmuring could be heard amongst them.

"You're gonna take Monster's spot in line. Starting now, all the lil' homies are your responsibility. You keep them in line, make sure they are all doing what the fuck they're supposed to be doing. Keep up that good shit, because muthafuckas are looking. Don't fuck up, though, homie, 'cause for now, you answer to me." Blinky's words didn't call for any sort of threat. Everyone already knew the consequences of fucking up.

"Whatever nonsense and shenanigans you fools are over here discussing is gone have to wait until mańana (tomorrow)." Blinky's old lady Jessica came walking up. "Right now, we supposed to be celebrating Monster, and I can't do no kind of celebrating without my papi (daddy)." She wrapped her arms around Blinky's waist and kissed his neck.

Jessica was a bad chick in every sense of the term. She was 5'8", 170 pounds of pure tits, hips, and ass. She had the looks that a muthafucka would kill for, and Blinky was always ready to do just that. Jessica was a light-skinned Mexican with hair that flowed down her back, which led to a huge, heart-shaped ass that Blinky better not catch you looking at. She grew up in the hood and earned the respect of both the homies and home girls from beating the shit out of bitches since she was young.

Blinky turned his head and gave his old lady a kiss. He broke the kiss off and addressed Chino again. "Get at me on Monday so we can go over some shit." Then he turned to address the rest of the homies. "You fools make sure y'all on yo' shit and make the homies look good. Hogg Status, fools!"

All of the homies called out 21st and made their hood call.

"Chino, congratulations, honey. It's your time to shine. Make sure you take full advantage of every opportunity you get, because you may not get too many." Jessica winked at Chino. Then she pulled Blinky away from the group.

"Congratulations, fool!" Now you're the Big Dawg!" Tyson was the first to call out his approval of Chino's promotion.

His congratulations were followed by all the rest of the homies. Chino heard and accepted all the praise from the homies, even though his attention was on that phat ass that Jessica had as he openly watched her and Blinky walk away. Chino couldn't help but to wonder what it would feel like to slide his dick between her phat, soft ass cheeks. Jessica and Blinky were about eight to ten feet away when she looked over her shoulder and caught Chino staring at her ass. To Chino's surprise, she licked her lips and winked at him.

Smokey, Chino's best friend since grade school, walked up to him and dropped his arm around Chino's shoulder and whispered in his ear, "It's our time, bitch!"

Chino smiled at his best friend's comment and without looking at him, said, "You muthafuck'n right."

De'Kari

Chapter 15

"Rogue, I don't know why you constantly wanna keep taking risks and doing stupid shit. Nigga, the money starting to come like crazy and we done kicked the muthafuck'n door all the way open. But you wanna take penitentiary chances by fucking wit' dummies!" Skrew was mad as fuck.

He was supposed to be on his way to the studio. Instead, he was at Shark Montana's trap spot helping him wipe down a case of Dracos that Shark was getting ready to take to Lil' Dooka. He couldn't understand the stupidity that Shark continued to display. But Shark was his big homie, more like big brother, and Skrew wasn't about to leave him hanging.

"See, there you go, nigga." Shark put down the Draco that was in his hand and picked up a plate that had an ounce of fire powder cocaine on it. "I told you that this is one of my lil' niggaz. When I was locked up in the county for fighting that case, me and the little nigga hit it off something cool. Nigga had my back when I had to rock up on some South City niggaz. So now that he beat that case for that mall shooting at Tan Fran (Tanforan Mall), he may need my help. I'm not about to leave the little nigga hanging. So, don't let that bother you." Shark scooped up a small hill of the coke and snorted it.

"Plus, if he wasn't out to support us at the show the other night, he wouldn't be in this funk to begin with. So, it's like I owe the nigga. Saut-te-tey!" Shark whipped his wrist in the air like he was a French baker whipping up a cake. Then he started laughing.

Truth was, Shark lived for the bullshit. Everything he told Skrew was true. Yet, even if it weren't, he would still be getting ready to do this because he loved being in the mix. He was the poster child for violence. A real party animal. He loved to party and have fun, yet the beast shit was embedded in him. That was that Stone Nation Taliban shit that was embedded deep into his soul.

"Nigga, I fully understand all of that loyalty shit. But, Rogue, we got muthafuckas that would've handled that shit for a nigga. Fuck we in here taking chances for?" Skrew sat down that last Draco that he just finished wiping down.

Skrew wasn't arguing or debating with Shark because he was a coward and scared. Not in the least. He at one time was heavy in the field also. During the height of the Taliban and Village Mobb war back in the day, a young Skrew stayed giving them Village niggaz the blues. In fact, it was Shark who nagged at Skrew over pursuing a career in rap after hearing his lil' homie spit some fire one night, when they were chilling at Skrew's trap in Menlo. Now the proverbial tables had changed, and it was Skrew trying to get Shark to see the light. He was trying to get Shark to leave the streets for good and embrace the rap hustle with both arms.

"Nigga, I done told you three times not to let that shit bother you. I can make this run down the way-way bolo. Ain't nothing 'bout to happen to the Shark. Niggaz already know what time it is wit' Shark Montana! Saut-te-tey, nigga!" The cocaine racing through his veins had Shark lightweight wishing something went wrong.

"Like I told you every other time you said that fuck nigga shit, Rogue, you got me fucked up! Everybody know dem Frisco niggaz are back door specialists. We already lost Stone in dat bitch. I ain't losing another one of my niggaz in that city!" Skrew reached for his Glock .23 and inspected it before placing it on his waist.

Stone Cold was a founding member of the Taliban who was set up and lost his life one night in San Francisco after going to the club. Shit ain't been the same since in East Palo Alto nor Menlo Park. Stone's death changed a lot of shit and fucked up a lot of niggaz.

Shark tucked both of his Glocks on his waist and smiled at Skrew. "Then don't let that bother you. Let's go, nigga."

The two of them carried the case and put it in the back of Shark's Tahoe. Shark left the plate of cocaine in the trap. It didn't matter, though, because he had two ounces inside the truck.

Saut-te-tey, muthafucka!

***

Chico pulled up to Blinky's house. He thought about calling Blinky to let him know he was outside before walking up to the house, then decided against it. Chino didn't want the older gangsta thinking he held full authority over him. He would give Blinky enough respect and authority over him to make Blinky think he was being a good little soldier and was falling in line like everyone thought he should.

Muthafuckas were in for a rude awakening!

Chino checked his 9mm before putting it on his waist. He was getting out of his car when an idea came to his mind. He dug in his pocket for his phone, fucked with it for a moment, and then put it back in his pocket. Chino figured he was going to record every conversation he had with Blinky. He didn't know if or when he may need some leverage over him.

When Chino got out of his car and double checked the address, he realized that he had actually parked in front of the house next door to Blinky's. As he walked next door to the correct house, he thought he saw the blinds move in the house. Like most of the houses on the street and in San Francisco, this was an old two-story row house. Judging by the look of it, the house was in bad need of repairs.

Chino walked up to the front door and knocked. "Come on in, Chino!" a female's voice called from inside.

Chino checked the doorknob. It was open. He pushed the door open and entered the house. Immediately, the smell of home-cooked Mexican food greeted his nose. Surprisingly, the inside of the house looked completely different than the outside. Everything was in clean and good condition. Most of the furniture looked new. There were two new brown leather sofas. They were the main furniture pieces. An end table was positioned on either side of the sofas. Across the far side of the living room was some sort of shrine to the Virgin Mary. To the left of that, directly in the center of the wall, hung a 65" Sony flatscreen TV. Even the front carpet was nice and thick.

Off to the left of the living room came the sounds of pots and pans clinking. Chino figured Jessica was in the kitchen whipping up something for dinner. He closed the door and took a seat, wondering where Blinky had gotten the expensive leather sofas from. As he began to pay more attention to the things in the front room, Jessica came walking in holding a cold bottle of Corona in her right hand.

She was wearing some sort of sheer blouse that did very little to conceal the big 44 DDs that were underneath it. The material was so light it was virtually see-through. Chino could see her titties as clear as he could if she had on nothing. Her skirt barely came down to mid-thigh. With the slit it had going up the side, the bottom half of her right ass cheek was fully exposed every time she took a step. Long, thick, firm legs went on forever.

Instantly, Chino's dick became hard at the sight of Jessica. He thought Blinky clearly had to be an idiot to allow her to walk around like this knowing he had company coming over.

His eyes hadn't even made it to her face yet. He couldn't bring himself to stop staring at her large strawberry nipples.

"Blinky said to tell you that he got held up. He's forty-five minutes away, stuck in traffic. But he said to make sure that you don't leave because he has something for you. Told me to tell you to get comfortable and make yourself at home until he gets here." She handed him the bottle of Corona that was in her hand.

The boldness in which he openly stared at her tits made Jessica's pussy tingle. She loved a pandillero (gangsta). She needed danger in her life. Needed to flirt with disaster, which was why she was attracted to Blinky. He stayed on edge and was always into shit. The problem was, as they had gotten older, his status elevated. Blinky got into less and less shit. She loved him to death, but her need for excitement was killing her. She needed a thrill worse than a junky needed an early morning fix.

"You see something you like, Chino?" Her question caught Chino off guard. Then he realized he was still staring at those nipples. They were fucking huge. He stared so long because he was imagining sucking on them.

Catching himself and quickly regaining his composure, Chino took a step back, and Jessica boldly took a step forward. She pressed her huge breasts up in his face. Her nipples poked up against Chino's chest. The contact sent a small electrical pulse through her body.

"Jessica, I don't know what the fuck you and this fool got going on, but I ain't the one for no fucking games." He tried to appear stern, but Chino knew she could feel his hard dick as she pressed up against him.

"Does it look like I'm playing games, Chino?" she asked him as she boldly reached between the two of them and took ahold of his rock-hard dick. She licked her lips and got so close to his face that he could smell the tequila on her breath. "Mmm. You wanna fuck me, don't you, Chino? Look how hard this dick is. I know you wanna taste this pinocha (pussy)."

Chino expected Blinky to come from out the back room or jump out of the front closet at any moment, ready to kill him.

"Look, ma, I'm not trynna disrespect the homie. Like I said, I don't know kind of shit you on, but you're barking up the wrong tree."

"Are you scared, Chino? Are you scared of Blinky?" She was purposely trying to push his buttons.

Before he could stop himself or even think about what he was doing, his hand shot out and took ahold of her neck. He wrapped his fingers tightly around her neck and squeezed harder.

"Bitch, I ain't scared of nobody!" he growled. Spit flew into her face.

"Mmm!" She wiggled against him as a wave of lust surfed through her body.

He saw that the rough shit was exciting her. Jessica's large strawberry nipples were hard against him. Even the grip she had on his dick tightened.

"Bitch, I told you to stop playing wit' me. Since you think it's a game, bitch, I'mma show you. Fuck you and Blinky." He was squeezing her neck so tight Jessica could barely breathe. She loved it. "Bitch, get on your knees and suck my dick!"

It was an order. He removed his hand from around her throat and forced her down on her knees. Then, after setting the Corona on one of the end tables, he pulled his dick out of his pants and shoved it down her throat. She just sat there on her knees with his dick in her mouth, not doing anything.

"Bitch, I said suck my dick!" Chino slapped her hard across the face. The sting got her attention.

Her mouth felt like a liquid volcano. Hot and super juicy! She began vigorously sucking Chino's dick. The smacking wet sounds her mouth made turned him on even more than the fact that he had seven inches of dick shoved deep down his big homie's girl's throat.

Jessica's left hand stroked Chino's dick while she sucked it. His right hand found her hot, wet pussy. It was so wet, it felt like she had peed on herself. The excitement was exhilarating. What if Blinky walked in on them? He would kill Chino for sure. She had made up the lie about Blinky being in traffic. The truth was, she had no idea where he was. He hadn't come home last night. The thought of him walking in on them caused her to cum right away.

Once the orgasm passed, the extent of what they were actually doing slapped her in the face harder than Chino had. If Blinky did walk in on them, he would kill her right along with Chino.

She spat Chino's dick out of her mouth and stood up off her knees.

"Huh, w-what the fuck is you doing, bitch? I was just about to cum!" He just knew this bitch was not about to try and play him.

"Chino, we can't do this. I don't know what the fuck I was thinking. What if Blinky walks in and catches us?" She started to walk away, but Chino caught her by the shoulders and spun her around so that she was facing him.

"What? Bitch, I'm not trynna hear none of that Blinky shit! Fuck Blinky! You got yo' nutt,, bitch now get back on your knees and give me mine!" This bitch had Chino fucked up! He could feel precum oozing out of the head of his dick. She was going to get him off.

"Look, muthafucka! I don't know who the fuck you putting your fucking hands on. I told yo' thirsty ass that Blinky is on his way back. That shit we just pulled was all the way fucked up! Yo' ass is lucky I did stop, 'cause if Blinky would've walked in and caught you wit' yo' dick down my throat, he would've fucked yo' little ass up and I would've just told him you forced me! Now I suggest you get out of my face and out my fucking house before I tell him anyway just so he fucks you up!" Jessica snatched away from Chino, spun around, and started to storm out of the living room.

"Thirsty." Chino repeated the word, dumbfounded.

He couldn't believe what the fuck she had just said to him. How in the fuck was he thirsty when the bitch was the one pushing all up on him? She had the nerve to call him a pussy by insinuating he was scared of Blinky.

With lightning speed, he reached out and snatched a handful of her hair. Jessica let out a loud yelp as Chino snatched her backward. She tried to fight to break his grasp, but it was useless.

"You think I'm scared of Blinky, bitch? Think I give a fuck if that nigga walked in?" He forcefully pushed her down

111

by her head. making her bend over the sofa. The small skirt rode up her ass, revealing that she wasn't wearing any panties.

The sight of her bare, juicy ass exposed in front of him caused his dick to throb. He smacked her on her ass cheeks. Her ass jiggled like Jell-O. Jessica was still talking shit and struggling to get free, yet she couldn't control the excitement that she was feeling. He learned over her until his lips were inches away from her ear.

"Bitch, when you tell that nigga how my dick tastes, make sure you tell him how good it felt too!" In one forceful motion, he rammed all seven inches of his rock-hard dick as deep into her soaking pussy as it would go.

It took all of Jessica's will not to scream out.

Chino let out a grunt of satisfaction. He knew this bitch had some good pussy. It was fire! His right hand was forcing Jessica's head down and holding her in place. As he fucked her hard, he smacked her ass repeatedly with his left hand. Talking shit while he fucked her.

"You…make…sure…he…knows…how…good…this…dick…is!" With every word he fucked her harder and harder. Her ass smacked loudly against him.

Jessica couldn't believe she was getting raped in Blinky's living room. Couldn't believe that Chino had the balls to violate her with no regard like this. Before she knew it, she was moaning loudly from the pleasure and excitement. Chino's big dick felt wonderful ramming into her. So much so that she exploded all over his dick.

That drove her wild. Jessica began throwing her ass back, violently attacking the dick. That shit was driving Chino crazy! Here he was taking the pussy, trying to teach the bitch a lesson, and she was enjoying it. He wanted to keep going. The pussy felt too good to stop, but he had a point to prove. Reluctantly, he pulled out of the pussy. Without hesitation, he rammed his dick deep into her ass. Jessica couldn't control it, she screamed out. Chino didn't give a fuck. He relentlessly fucked her in her ass just as hard as he fucked her pussy. Her asshole was so tight he had to close his eyes to savor the shit.

Once the initial pain wore off, getting fucked in her ass was the best feeling Jessica had ever felt. She couldn't stop cumming. She was cumming out her pussy and her ass at the same time. She'd always wanted Blinky to fuck her in her big ass, but he wouldn't do it. He would tell her that was some faggot shit. To Blinky, only homosexuals wanted to fuck people in the ass.

When Chino couldn't hold out any longer, he shot a big wad deep into her asshole. He was panting like a wild animal. The nutt felt so good he bent over her and stayed that way for a minute. He couldn't care less if Blinky walked in right then. Chino would just fill him with some hot shit like he just did his bitch. He pumped into her ass two more times, making sure to leave every drop of nutt inside of her.

When he pulled out of her ass, his nutt spilled out. Fixing himself back inside his pants, he told her, "Now make sure you tell that nigga how good the dick was."

She was still bent over the couch with her naked ass in the air when Chino walked out of the house. He didn't even bother closing the door after himself.

Chapter 16

2:47 pm

The busy streets of Haight and Ashbury were crowded as usual. It was one of San Francisco's most famous tourist attractions. Every year the city brought in millions of dollars off tourism in Haight and Ashbury. It's a wonder why the closest police stations were miles away. The closest being the Southeast station in Golden Gate Park. The second closest police station was located all the way in Pacific Heights, which might as well be light years away, it was so far.

These two police stations just happened to also be the closest stations to San Francisco's Inner Richmond District, which was next to Francisco Heights. The district that separated Inner Richmond from the Haight District, which was basically the Filmore District.

This all may sound confusing to outsiders, but to local San Franciscans, or as they call themselves, Frisconians, this knowledge was as elementary as riding a bike. Murda was a born and raised Frisconian thru and thru. He wasn't one of them niggas that stuck to just his hood growing up. He traveled the entire city. Shit, before all of the inner-city funk, Murda considered all of San Francisco his hood.

All of this played a part in the planning of today's events. Because of his vast knowledge of the entire city's intricate dealings, Murda knew that officers patrolled this section regularly. It was a part of the officer's beat.

The blistering sun rays took little effect on the homeless man wrapped in the many wool blankets that passersby steered clear of. There was always a steady breeze blowing off the Pacific Ocean that kept San Francisco blanketed in a cool breeze. It was this breeze that lessened the effects of the sun's rays.

No one paid attention to the homeless man who wasn't begging for change. The people didn't bother paying any attention to the leather backpack that rested in his lap, that was brand new. People definitely didn't notice when the homeless man checked his watch to see that it was 2:49 pm that the watch was too expensive for a homeless man to have. Their laxity would prove to be a fatal mistake on this day.

At 2:49 pm, the homeless man noticed the black and white color scheme of the patrol car that he had been wanting at this intersection for. As the patrol car came to a slow stop at the red light, Murda, who was dressed as the homeless man, rose from his spot.

People may not have given a fuck about the homeless black man who had been sitting on the corner, but they did, however, pay attention to the dark-skinned, thick-bearded black man that stood up with the assault rifle that he took out of the bag that was seated on his lap.

People began running before he even fired. The commotion drew the attention of the officer in the passenger seat of the patrol car. He turned his head to his right to see what all of the commotion was about. The white officer was a fifteen-year veteran on the force. He was well seasoned because he had seen plenty of action. However, he still nearly shit his pants at the sight of the black man holding the assault rifle pointed and trained directly on him. His partner, an African American, ten-year veteran on the force, never received the pleasure of knowing what hit them.

Murder placed his feet firmly underneath him. When the white officer looked in Murda's direction, Murda smiled and squeezed the trigger. The AK-47 roared thunderously in his hands. The massive 223s that spit from the barrel tumbled through the air, chopping up everything they came in contact with, including the squad car.

A female tourist who was walking down the street with her husband was scared so badly that she just stood where she was in shock, as urine ran down her leg forming a puddle underneath her red Jimmy Choos. Unfortunately for her, her husband, who abandoned her, was halfway down the street running for his life. He was too scared to dare glance back and see about his wife of eleven and a half years.

Murda kept his finger on the trigger and the assault rifle trained steady on his two targets until the firing pin landed on an empty clip. The carnage was devastating. Thirty-seven of the fifty 223s zipped through the now deceased body of the officer in the passenger seat. Twenty-six shredded the body of the driver. The patrol car sat at the stop light bullet riddled and smoking. It resembled a war-wrecked Hum-Vee in the battle grounds of Desert Storm.

Satisfied with his handywork, Murda turned around and ran down the alleyway next to where he had been sitting. Halfway down the alley, he wiped down the AK-47 before tossing it. He quickly stripped off the raggedy looking homeless clothes he wore over a business suit. A block away from the alleyway, he hopped into a four-door, grey Honda Accord and blended in with the rest of the traffic.

***

(2:51 pm)

XO sat in the passenger seat of the stolen Chevy Malibu. Dell and Don both were in the backseat while CJ sat behind the wheel in the driver's seat. CJ was the getaway driver. All four men's attention was on the police scanner that sat on the dashboard.

XO was sending suggestive thoughts and energy out into the universe, hoping that his younger brother, Murda, was okay. He knew his brother was about that action. He also knew there wasn't anything wrong with a little reinforcement in the form of positive thinking. XO wasn't a religious man, but he did believe in the laws of attraction and the laws governing "Positive Mental Thinking." His fingers gripped the

Mack 11 he had in his lap in full concentration and anticipation.

Finally, at 2:52 pm, it happened. "Attention all units! Attention all units! Code three! I repeat, this is a code three! We have reports of a 10-72, multiple shots fired at the intersection of Haight and Asbury. Again, multiple shots are reported at the intersection of Haight and Asbury. All units this is a 10-00, I repeat, this is a 10-00, you guys, officer down!" All units respond!" The dispatcher's words sent chills down the spine of everybody who heard the words, except for the four niggaz in the Malibu.

They waited ten full minutes, giving the all the police time to respond to the call before making their move.

"Let's get it!" XO pulled the Santa Claus mask down over his face. The others did the same thing.

No other words were spoken. Three Santa Clauses entered the San Francisco Federal Credit Union. Two of the three were carrying fully loaded automatic assault weapons in their hands.

Don was the first one through the door. As soon as he entered the doors, he smacked the 52-year-old security guard across the back of his head, cracking the back of his skull wide open from the amount of force he used.

Don never broke his stride. He continued straight to the tellers' counter as he yelled, "Everybody shut the fuck up and get the fuck on the ground!"

"Get the fuck down!" The sight of the 6'3", 200-pound Santa Claus holding the assault rifle and yelling the order to get down commanded everyone's attention.

Some of the civilians inside of the bank still screamed as they got down.

"Bitch, he said shut the fuck up!" XO punched an Asian woman, who just stood there screaming, on the left side of her jaw. The blow shattered her jawbone and sent her sprawling across the floor. Her unconscious body slid until it crashed up against the front of the bank tellers' counter. At the sight of

118

what happened to the Asian woman, everyone else quickly complied without further hesitation or incident. Fear was written on the faces of all the civilians as they closed their eyes and prayed that this was one great big nightmare. One that they would hopefully wake up from.

The security guard laid on the floor moaning. The pain from the head injury was excruciating.

The bank manager, an older white woman in her early fifties, was thinking heavily about taking the risk and reaching over toward her desk, which was roughly nine feet away from her, and pushing the alarm. When XO looked at her, she felt like he saw into her soul. "Bitch, don't think about trynna be a hero. I'll fill yo' bitch ass body full of holes."

To everyone inside of the bank, it was as if time stood still. It seemed that the altercation lasted forever. In reality, Don was done loading up all the cash accessible inside the bank in under two minutes. At 3:04 pm, he was rushing past Dell with a duffel bag full of cash.

Dell followed Don out the front door with XO pulling up the rear. They made their way to the Malibu, guns ready for whatever in case the police showed up. Once they all piled in, CJ pulled off. The address of the San Francisco Federal Credit Union was 4375 Geary Blvd. Instead of heading toward the freeway, the Malibu sped toward its next destination, which was 5498 Geary Blvd. It was the address of The Sterling Bank and Trust.

The tires screeched to a loud, burning stop in front of the bank. The street was fairly empty, so the car didn't attract that much attention. A UPS delivery man who was just finished making a delivery turned toward the sound of the screeching tires. What he saw made him decide to mind his own business and get the fuck back in his truck and out of the area. What he saw was three niggaz with Santa Claus masks on and Choppas in their hands.

The time was 3:10 pm when they entered the bank. Inside of the bank, everything happened much the same way as it did in the first bank. Only this time it went smoothly, with no one getting hurt.

By 3:14 pm, the silver Malibu was making its way to the third and final bank, The First Republic Bank at 6001 Geary Blvd. Right down the street from the first and second banks.

The call about the first bank robbery went out at 3:08 pm. The four of them listened to the call over the scanner as they raced toward the second bank. Just as CJ figured, with every cop in the surrounding three districts responding to the call about officers down, not a single cop responded to the bank robbery.

***

When the call about the second bank robbery went out over the radio at 3:15 pm, Sergeant Jerome Baker first thought dispatch was reissuing the call, due to no one responding to the first one. He was just walking into his favorite corner sandwich shop on his lunch break when he heard the first call. The second one came just as he was leaving the sandwich shop, climbing into his squad car.

It wasn't until dispatch came over the radio about the second robbery that Sergeant Baker realized something was wrong.

"Dispatch, this is #8547, what were the addresses on those two 211s?"

"Unit #8547, dispatch. The first at 3:11 pm a 211 in progress reported at 4375 Geary Blvd. Then again reports of a second 211 in progress has been reported at 5498 Geary Blvd., call came through at 3:15 pm."

"10-04, dispatch. #8547 responding to the first call. With everyone responding to the code three, it's likely that I'll be taking the second call as well."

"10-04, #8547. Both calls gave a description of a silver sedan as the getaway vehicle for both 211s."

Sergeant Baker started his car and sped off in the direction of the first bank robbery. "10-04, dispatch, my ETA is about five minutes."

"10-04." The dispatcher disconnected the call.

Even though Sergeant Baker was closer to the second reported robbery than the first, protocol stated that he was supposed to respond to the first call. As he pulled up to the intersection leaving the 5000 block of Geary Blvd., he could actually see the second bank in his rearview.

Just before he pulled off, his radio squeaked to life. "Unit #8547, this is dispatch. We just received a 10-72, shots fired during a 211 in progress at 6001 Geary Blvd. Repeat, 211 in progress at The First Republic Bank at 6001 Geary Blvd."

Sergeant Baker couldn't believe it. Three robberies in twenty minutes on the same street. Sergeant Baker didn't believe in coincidences. Cutting his siren on, he flipped a U-turn and sped back down Geary Blvd. in the direction of The First Republic Bank. He knew in his gut that all three bank robberies were connected, and all three were connected somehow to the 10-00 officer down. He was hell bent on catching the suspects in the act. They wouldn't get away with this shit in his city. Not if he could help it.

Chapter 17

The adrenaline and energy inside of the Malibu was so high it interfered with the radio signal on the police scanner. The static electricity was messing with the scanner's interface. All that meant to XO was the scanner was fucking up. It really didn't matter, though, they were seconds away from pulling up to their third and final bank.

Everything went off without a problem until the Mobb was exiting the bank. One of the bank customers happened to be a retired police officer turned private investigator licensed to carry a concealed firearm. He was a Hispanic man in his late forties. Though he was no longer a police officer, he was still plagued with the desire to want to be a hero.

Don had already exited the bank with two duffel bags full of money. As Don ran past Dell, one of the heavy duffel bags knocked into him. It caused Dell to stumble sideways a couple of steps. That's when all hell broke loose!

The retired police officer turned private investigator chose to take advantage of the hiccup and try to become a fucking hero. The next sequence of events would prove to be the ultimate downfall of the 357 Mobb.

The private investigator pulled his concealed 9mm from underneath his jacket. He fired from his position on the floor twice. The first bullet went wide, knocking out the bank's front window. The second slug slammed into Dell's chest, knocking him backward. Instantly, Dell squeezed the trigger of the assault rifle in his hands. A burst of bullets flew wildly from the tip of the barrel. Several of the bullets tore into a couple of the customers who were laid face down on the ground.

XO spun around the moment he heard the sound of gun fire. He turned in time to see Dell stumbling backward. When XO saw the private investigator holding the gun, he sent a furry of bullets his way with the squeeze of his finger. This gave the security guard the distraction he was looking for. The security guard quickly stood up and drew his service weapon. This was the first time he had ever seen anything close to action in the bank. He was scared shitless This caused him to pull the trigger too soon with shaky, unstable hands. The bullets he intended for XO didn't even come close to hitting the target. In fear of the bullets the security guard knew XO would send his way in retaliation, he hurriedly dove behind a wooden desk.

XO didn't return fire. Instead, he checked on Dell. The bullet that caught him in the chest didn't go any further than the Kevlar vest that XO was wearing. The guard let off two more shots from what he wrongfully assumed was a good hiding place. Dell, who had fully recovered by this point, aimed his assault rifle at the desk the guard was crouched behind and pulled the trigger. The desk jumped and rocked as the huge 223s put holes the size of lemons in the desk or knocked out entire chunks.

The screaming customers were in a panic. Two people had been brutally murdered right in front of them. Their screams and cries sailed through the air as Dell and XO finally made their way out of the bank. The few people who were on the street close enough to hear ran and hid for cover at the first sound of gunfire. Therefore, no one was around as they came running out of the bank. If anyone hadn't ran at the sound of gunfire, they surely disappeared from the sight of Don, who stood outside of the bank waiting in front of the Malibu holding the AR-15. The three bank robbers all piled into the Malibu, and CJ sped off.

The call had already gone out over the radio. As they sped toward the next spot where they had new cars waiting for them, no one said anything. They were paranoid. Of course, there were always hidden variables to take into consideration whenever planning something. However, no one was supposed to get hurt, yet they killed two people. If they were to get caught, they were facing the death penalty. Without question, they all would rather shoot it out on the streets. This was why everybody was on edge.

They made it to the switch spot a few blocks away and everybody got out. The switch cars were waiting for them. CJ jumped into the white Honda Civic. Don and Dell, whose chest was still hurting, hopped inside of a black Chevy Tahoe. While the three of them drove off in separate directions, XO poured gasoline all over the outside and inside of the Malibu. Then he set the car ablaze and jumped inside a tan Chevy Silverado with an *I voted for Trump!* sticker on the bumper and back window and drove off.

Looking at the clock as he drove away, it read 3:34 pm.

***

Sergeant Baker's car came to a screeching halt in front of the bank in the same exact spot the Malibu just drove off from a minute and twelve seconds before. Sergeant Baker's instincts told him that he was too late. Yet, he still proceeded with caution.

The first thing he noticed was the front windows of the bank that had been shot out. His trained nose immediately picked up on the scent of burnt sulfur, the unmistakable smell of gun powder. Sergeant Baker pulled his service weapon while scanning the area outside of the bank. Not seeing anything or anyone that looked out of place or suspicious, he made his way inside of the bank.

The stench of gun powder got stronger once he was inside the bank. The cries of the wounded found his ears just about the same time as his eyes found them on the ground. A few customers and bank employees were doing what they could to aid the wounded.

"San Francisco Police Department!" He made his presence known as a cautionary method, in case there were any trigger-happy good Samaritans amongst the group.

At the sound and sight of a law enforcement officer, a wave of relief washed over the surviving bank customers. All at once, people began shouting off things to him. He was used to the behavior of survivors of violent encounters. While keeping a trained ear out in case someone used words that would suggest importance, his eyes were also trained so they took in as much as they could.

"Dispatch, this is #8547. I'm 10-30 at The First Republic Bank. I'm going to need a few buses. We have multiple injured. From the looks of it, I'd say gunshot victims, possibly from a high-powered assault rifle of some sort." He sidestepped what he knew from experience was an already dead body. He made his way to the bullet-riddled desk. "And you might as well notify the coroner, looks to me that we have a couple of DOAs. Unfortunately, we have another 10-00. Looks like the security guard."

"Copy that, #8547. All units in the vicinity of The First Republic Bank on the six-thousand block of Geary, we have an officer involved shooting during an apparent 211. 10-00, officer down. I repeat, 10-00, officer down. #8547, emergency personnel notified. Two buses have been alerted and are in route to your location, as well as notification to the coroner's office."

A woman who had the look and aura of the bank manager approached Sergeant Baker. "Um, excuse me, Officer, my name is Caroline Harper, I am the bank manager. I'll be able and willing to answer any questions you may have. It was God awfully horrible."

Sergeant Baker holstered his weapon and removed a pen and notepad. Next, he grabbed his tape recorder out of his pocket. He then pressed record and began going over Caroline Harper's statement. It was going to be a very long evening.

Chapter 18

"De'Mario, please listen to me, baby. I hear what you're saying, but you don't have to do this. Baby, please. I'm okay and you are okay. You don't have to do anything further. Baby, please, I'm scared something may happen to you in the process of you seeking revenge. Baby, just leave it all in God's hands. Everything will be okay." G-Baby was very upset.

She woke up just over ten minutes ago and overhead a conversation C1ty was having with one of his cousins. As soon as he had gotten off the phone, she questioned him about what she had heard. Not one to lie to her, C1ty told G-Baby about the plans he had for the muthafuckas who shot at them at the club. G-Baby couldn't believe what C1ty told her. Not just the things they had done already since that night at the club, but the things that he had planned for the niggaz that shot them, sent chills down G-Baby's spine.

She had come out of her coma two and a half weeks ago, and C1ty was right there by her side. Last week the doctors agreed to release her and allow C1ty to take her home, under the orders that she was to get plenty of sleep and remain stress free.

C1ty walked over to the bed and sat down facing G-Baby and stared her in her eyes. Tears began to fall from them. He reached out and gently wiped the tears away. He didn't want to see his baby cry, but he wasn't about to lie to her either. As far as C1ty was concerned, every member of TIO was living on borrowed time.

"Genesis, I need you to listen to me and think rationally while you're doing so. You can't allow your emotions to interfere because emotions will cloud your judgement, okay? Can you do that for me, baby?" C1ty desperately hoped he could get through to her. G-Baby nodded her head yes in response and fought back her tears.

"I didn't ask for what happened to happen. Lord knows I didn't. But it did. Now I reacted out of emotions that I am not ashamed of. I will do what I did all over again in a heartbeat. I need you to understand that there is no way them guys can let what we did go unanswered for. Not in this jungle. You can believe that they are getting ready to come for us because they have to. The streets won't allow them to do anything else. Now, I would be a fool to allow us to sit back and wait for those niggaz to get at us. Ain't no telling what will pop off if I did. The only choice that I have is to keep hitting them hard, until there is nobody left to hit. Or else they're going to make sure that there ain't no more of us to hit them. I need for you to trust me on this one, baby."

"But what if you're wrong? What if things don't go the way that you want them to? Then what, De'Mario? Huh? What am I supposed to do if something happens to you?" A fresh wave of tears fell from her eyes as she cried openly, afraid for her man.

He leaned forward and kissed away her tears. "Baby, nothing is going to happen to me."

"Can you promise me that?" G-Baby wasn't doubting C1ty nor his ability to take care of himself. She had grown up in the hood and often saw what the streets could do. She knew what they were capable of.

C1ty knew what she was asking was virtually impossible. Nearly nothing in life was guaranteed, especially when you were in the field. The streets were a cold jungle. G-Baby had her own set of rules governed by unwritten laws, which meant at any given moment of any given day, anything could happen.

"G-Baby, you know I can't promise you that. Just like I can't promise nothing could happen to me simply walking to the store. What I can and I will promise you, is that I will always be on my toes. Thinking and re-analyzing the shit that we come up with, in order to make sure that I stay as safe as possible. I promise you this, baby, it will take an army to take me away from you!" The sincerity in which he spoke pulled at the strings of her heart.

She knew he was trying his best to avoid her question. Because deep down, she knew herself that she was asking him something that he couldn't promise. She was looking for the comfort of guarantee, security that he just couldn't give her. The fucked-up thing was, deep in her heart, G-Baby knew everything he spoke was truth. He had no choice. They left him no option the moment the first shots rang out! He had to take it to them Tear It Off niggaz before they brought it to him.

"De'Mario, you know that I know the rules to this shit. It doesn't mean that I have to like them or be okay with them. But I know the rules. You just better make sure that you do what you said you would do. I don't care about nothing and nobody but you. You make sure that while you run through them jungles, you do so intending to bring your ass back to me." G-Baby hugged her man as tight as she could, while the tears fell freely. "I love you, De'Mario!"

C1ty held G-Baby tightly in his arms for a long time before tenderly kissing her on the lips. She was the only thing in life that mattered to him, and he needed her to know it. His tender kisses became passionate, and before long, he was making slow, sweet love to her. Pouring out all the emotions he couldn't verbally get out. Doing his best to show her how much she meant to him.

When they went to sleep in each other's arms that night, neither of them had any way of knowing that along with the new day, the morning sun was about to open the gates of Hell into their lives.

***

(Earlier that day)

"Brah, what the fuck you mean don't let that bother me? Nigga, it ain't bothering me. I'm saying, though, Shark, how much you want for these muthafuckas?" Lil' Dooka was looking at the guns that Shark and Skrew brought him.

He couldn't understand the logic behind Shark just giving him the weapons. He was too young to understand the code that Shark lived by. Nowadays they lived by pay your way. Everything they did was in the name of the bag, which the youngstas chased religiously. Shark Montana was from a different era. He lived and would die for loyalty. That meant if he fucked with you, he fucked with you. No ifs, ands, or buts about it. If he was down with you, he was all the way down with you... Not sometimes, not halfway.

"I'm saying, lil' nigga, don't let that bother you. When you fuck wit' Shark Montana, if I'm eating, then you eating! If you beef'n, then I'm beef'n! Straight up, ain't no two ways about this shit. The only thing you need to do is let me know if you got this shit. Or do I need to bring the Ban through dis bitch." One phone call was all it would take for Shark to have an entire squad of Taliban niggaz ready to slide thru and body some shit.

"What! Come on, nigga, how you sound? Shark, this Tear It Off, nigga! We got this shit. That's on BR!" Lil' Dooka appreciated the gesture, but what did he look like asking for or accepting some help solving his own problems. That's that nerd shit!

"Let me know that shit then. Well then, you know as they say, time is money. I gotta go see about my cash so I ain't gotta put my foot up a hoe's ass. Saut-te-tey, muthafucka!" Back in the day, people would've referred to Shark as a gangsta mack because he played with guns and he played with hoes. Today, though, everything was pimp'n, at least to some, and Shark Montana was one.

Shark made his way back over to the parking spot where Skrew was waiting for him with his Mack-11 cocked and ready on his lap. He didn't take it off of his lap until he had driven a good quarter mile away from the Lowes parking lot they had just left.

130

Chapter 19

Later that same night

Behind the tinted windows of the Porsche Cayenne truck, Wes felt like a million dollars. Being third in command of the 357 Mobb didn't really mean shit to him. At the end of the day, they were all family and treated each other the way that family members treated each other. The only person who really wielded any authority was C1ty, and that was because they all not only loved him, but they also respected his mind. C1ty was the most analytical and calculating of all of them.

Most niggaz craved and coveted power, but not Wes. Money made the world go round and Wes was a part of that world. At twenty years old, money was one of his top priorities. Thanks to C1ty and his ingenius, ideas they were all swimming in money. They all knew that they couldn't go around spending their money, but just knowing they had it was enough for Wes. Wes knew that he had enough money to make sure he never had money problems. All he had to do was make sure he didn't fuck his money off.

The plan that they set forth for all of them to follow was simple. They were going to rob twenty of San Francisco's banks in a year's time. In that year, they would only spend what was needed to survive. Afterwards, they would put San Francisco and California in their rearview. So far, the plan was looking good and Wes was loving it. He glanced over toward his passenger seat, and the smile that was on his face got even bigger. Rayna tended to have that effect on people. She was a 5'9", 205-pound Black and Samoan beauty. One hundred ninety-five pounds of it was all tits and ass. To sweeten the deal, she had one of those faces that a nigga wouldn't mind staring at for hours.

Rayna was a stripper at The Century off O'Farrell and Larkin in San Francisco. In fact, she was one of the club's main attractions. She and Wes hit it off one night a little while back after he stumbled into The Century looking to blow off a little steam. When he saw her perform, he knew he had to have her. The way she slithered and moved her body on top of that stage was mind blowing.

He instantly requested a lap dance after her performance. Seeing her up close and personal, he realized she was thicker than he had thought. The sight of her juicy thighs jiggling as she made her way over to his both had his dick rock hard by the time she made it over to him. They talked and got to know each other while she worked her magic. One dance turned into another, which led to another. Without realizing it, they talked, laughed, and flirted with each other her entire shift, with her only taking a break in between to go back up on stage for her second performance. This time while she was up on the stage, it felt to Wes like she was personally dancing just for him. The two of them never broke eye contact the entire time she was on the stage. Their eyes played a sensual, tantalizing game built on the energy of raw sexual desire.

When her shift was over, he offered to take her out to breakfast where they could continue to connect and get to know one another more. He was shocked and disappointed when she turned down his offer. To Wes, the offer was just that, simply an offer. To Rayna, it was an invitation to so much more, and she didn't rock like that. Declining his offer, she elected to give him her number, which he accepted.

The two had been talking on the phone regularly ever since. Twice, they arranged to hook up. However, both times something came up, causing them to postpone and reschedule. Tonight, they were finally able to hook up without any issues.

"Damn, girl, you ain't put that phone down since you climbed into the whip. Let me find out you got a stalker for a baby daddy and you gotta check in every ten minutes," Wes said jokingly, trying to draw her attention away from all the texting she was doing.

"Boy, please! How you sound? For one, I don't have no kids, and even if I did, I sure wouldn't be checking in with some nigga. The only time I punch the clock is at the club. That way, a nigga can't toy and play me out my chicken (money). Anyway, my sister is going through something with her dude right now and I'm just trying to be there for her." Even while she spoke, Rayna's manicured fingers tapped away on her phone.

"Yeah, okay. You go right on ahead and play Doctor Phil or whatever it is you say you're doing. But I'm letting you know now, if two big San Quentin parolee looking mutha-fuckas kick in the door while we're doing our thing tonight, I'm shooting your ass first before I even think about sending some hot shit their way." Wes said it jokingly, but he was low-key letting her know that he wasn't game goofy.

Rayna caught the underlying seriousness in his joke, but she wasn't stunting it.

"Damn! That's fucked up. You would really shoot a bitch?" She placed her phone on her lap and played like she was offended. "I thought we were better than that, Wes."

"If you were trynna set a nigga up, then apparently we wasn't that cool to begin with. So, I might as well blow your shit off for toying with a nigga's heart," Wes joked back with her.

Rayna leaned over and lightly stroked his chest. Then she whispered flirtatiously, "Wes, are you trying to tell me that you're willing to give me your heart?" she purred in his ear.

Wes smiled. "I'm thinking about giving you a part of me right now, but it ain't my heart."

"Oh, really?" Rayna let her hand slide down the front of him until it rested on his lap. She could see the bulge of his rising dick through his pants. "Well, let's just see about that." She unzipped his pants and pulled his dick out.

At the sight of his dick in her hand, Rayna's mouth began to water. Rayna loved sucking dick. The feel of a nice, meaty, rock-hard dick throbbing inside of her mouth while she sucked on it, drove her crazy. She lowered her head and kissed the tip of his dick before opening her mouth and hungrily devouring it. She made the entire shaft disappear.

That shit felt so good, Wes almost crashed into a red Mustang as he was pulling into the parking lot of the Embassy Suites off Grand Avenue. When he swerved to miss the Mustang, Rayna smiled. She stopped what she was doing , satisfied that she'd gotten his attention. She still had the smile on her face when she put his wet dick back inside of his pants.

Wes kicked himself in the ass mentally for making the rookie mistake. He kept it playa, though, and remained smooth. In his mind, he was thinking if the head was that good there was no telling how crazy her pussy game was. From the way her ass was shaking as she made her way across the parking lot to the main lobby, he had a feeling that he was in store for a real treat. Images of her working her body on the stage came to his mind, as if to confirm his thoughts.

Rayna didn't have to look to see if he was checking her ass out, she could feel his eyes burning holes through the back of her yoga pants. Of course, this made her step like a true thoroughbred stallion. Her ass cheeks hypnotically swayed and jumped like they were made of Jell-O. After retrieving the key card to room 428, they made their way to the elevator. She didn't event wait for the elevator doors to close before she attacked him with hungry, breathtaking kisses. Wes didn't give a fuck that her mouth was just filled with his dick moments before, he matched her kisses, passion for passion. By the time they finally made it to the room, they both were almost undressed.

***

Reco, T.G., and MoMo, sat in the back room at Auntie Dee's spot playing *Call of Duty*, *Search and Destroy Mode*, on the PS4. They'd been at it for over an hour. They were just killing time until the phone call that Reco was waiting on the came through.

Reco and T.G. were heavily into the game, but MoMo was starting to get pissed off waiting for the bitch. He didn't have any understanding and zero patience. MoMo was ready to knock some shit down. Period!

A knock came at the door, but there was no need to ask who it was. Auntie Dee was the only person that ever knocked on the door. All the niggaz just walked in. She knocked because she liked to give them their privacy. Auntie Dee was MoMo, Turk, Nardy, and T.G.'s real aunt, but the entire clique called her Auntie. Her apartment was also their main hangout.

"Come in, Auntie," Reco called out. Auntie Dee opened the door. She stood in the doorway in a pair of dark grey sweats and an old red 49er T-shirt.

"Boys, I need a few dollars 'cause I got some shit that I need to take care of and I don't have any money."

"How much you need?" T.G. asked with no hesitation while holding his controller in one hand and reaching in his pocket with the other.

"A couple of hundred." She said this as naturally as she would have if she was asking for three dollars.

Reco started laughing. "Got damn, Auntie! Since when they start calling a couple hundred a few dollars?" MoMo and T.G. laughed at the joke as well.

"Shit, sobrino (nephew), since I'm the one asking y'all for the money instead of you asking me. Now since you got jokes and shit, why don't you do like T.G. and reach into them pockets. Especially since you always the one eating up everything." She crossed her arms over her ample breasts and leaned against the door jam in a *nigga try me if you want to* manner.

"Yeah, big mouth!" T. G. chimed in.

Reco paused the game, and all three of them reached into their pockets and tore her off two hundred a piece.

"Thank you, babies." Happily, Auntie Dee closed the door. Grateful to her nephews for the six hundred they just gave her. She grabbed her Newports and went out back to have a smoke.

When Auntie Dee left, Reco picked the controller up and resumed the game. Not even ten seconds later, the sound of his phone's text message alert chimed. MoMo looked over at Reco, waiting. A smile the size of Kansas spread across Reco's face as he read the text message. "Alright, bitches, that was it. Let's go make this shit happen!"

"On B. R., nigga let's get it!" T.G. agreed.

MoMo didn't say shit. He didn't have to. They all knew what time it was.

Chapter 20

Once they made it inside the room, Wes took control. He pinned Rayna up against the wall. He held her hands in the air above her head and began kissing her like his life depended on it. Her juicy lips held their own against his assault. Keeping her hands pinned, he broke the kiss and began biting and kissing on her neck, leaving monkey bites everywhere his mouth went.

Rayna's lil' pussy was on fire. His aggression and hunger had her beyond turned on. She gasped excitedly when Wes savagely tore her sheer blouse open. The buttons flew everywhere when they popped off. Rayna moaned so intensely when Wes began sucking one of her tits with his fiery mouth. As he sucked and nibbled on her big nipple, his other hand gripped both of her ass cheeks roughly. Rayna didn't even bother dropping her arms once Wes released his grip. She couldn't. The shit was feeling too good! The loud slurping sounds Wes was making as he popped one tit out of his mouth and attacked the next one, added to the tingling in her pussy.

Wes let go of her left ass check and slid his right hand down the front of her yoga pants in search of her pussy. He couldn't believe how phat that muthafucka was. He could literally palm her pussy with his hand. She was so excited the heat from her bald pussy instantly warmed his hand. He grabbed both of her huge pussy mounds, then squeezed.

"Wes, oh my god," she moaned as two of his fingers slipped inside of her overflowing pussy. After tickling her insides for a minute, his searching finger found her enlarged, pulsating clit. At the same moment, he bit down on her nipple. She shook violently as an orgasm tore through her body.

"Oh my fucking goodness," she screamed out as her head involuntarily knocked against the wall.

Wes didn't let up. Not even when her legs began quaking. His fingers continued their assault on her clit. While he continued to finger her, Wes raised his head and found her mouth again. She welcomed him eagerly. Her hips began slowly winding. Just when Rayna was really getting into it, he broke their contact and stripped her out of her yoga pants. Her panties couldn't get in his way because she didn't have any on.

He took a step back to admire her thickness. Her pussy was so pretty and phat that he wanted to get down on his knees immediately and suck on that juicy muthafucka, but Wes wasn't about to play himself like that. He was feeling her but wasn't about to be on no sucka shit. Instead, he tore his clothes off like they were on fire.

When Rayna saw the size of his dick once he was standing completely naked, she knew that she was about to get her brains fucked out. Silently, she thanked God. She opened her mouth to say something but never got the chance because he rushed her, kissing her powerfully and demandingly. Again, he reached down and grabbed both ass checks, this time picking her up.

"Put that muthafucka in there," he growled into her mouth while staring intensely in her eyes.

Rayna was more than happy to comply with the demand. What she wasn't ready for was Wes' dick game. He fucked her so hard up against the wall the pictures started falling down and the people next door began to bang on the wall.

Rayna couldn't help herself. She screamed over and over at the top of her lungs. Wes was putting a severe beating on the pussy and she loved every second of it. When he finally came, she dug her long-manicured nails into his back. He shoved his dick so deep into her pussy that she thought she would split. The sensation triggered a massive orgasm to erupt. Although she had lost track of how many orgasms she had, Rayna knew that was at least number five.

Wes waited until his nuts were completely drained before carrying her over to the couch. His dick remained rock hard and never fell out as he walked. Both of their naked bodies were covered in sweat. As Wes walked, cool air brushed against their bodies. The coolness was welcomed and refreshing. He sat down still inside of her.

Rayna instantly began riding him like a wild mare in heat. Her ass cheeks clapped loudly against his thighs as she bounced and bucked. Juices ran out her pussy, down the shaft of his dick, and covered his balls. Wes grabbed a handful of her hair and pulled her head back. Then, like a thirsty vampire, he attacked her neck. She was overwhelmed with pleasure, and tears started falling from her eyes. The salty taste of her perspiration was like candy to his taste buds. They were going at it so hard that the couch began rocking as Rayna's cries of pleasure grew louder.

Twenty-five minutes later, Rayna's body was drenched with sweat when she finally collapsed on top of Wes. He'd just shot another stream of nutt into her sore pussy. She was ready for a nice shower and a good night's sleep, but Wes had other plans. They took a shower, where he attacked her again under the hot water. They finished with her bent over the bathroom sink, and him mesmerized by her massive ass cheeks as they clapped while he fucked her.

After another hot shower, he took her to the king-size bed where he put her to sleep by making slow, sweet love to her. The experience was one she would remember for the rest of her life. She finally drifted off to sleep sometime after 1 am.

They were both awakened at 1:52 am by the sound of Rayna's cell phone that wouldn't stop ringing. She climbed out of the cozy bed, dirt tired and ready to murder whoever was blowing her phone up. Her anger quickly subsided once she looked at her screen and saw she had twenty-five text messages, all from the same person. The last few remnants of anger that remained dissipated the moment she began reading the first text message. Each message was worse than the one before. By the fourth message, she had read more than enough. She walked back over to the bed and shook Wes.

"Look, I know I said I would kill you first once the San Quentin crew came, but you felt so good. Tell them niggaz they can have everything, just let me keep you."

Rayna thought he would be pissed off, but when she explained what was going on, Wes was very understanding and compassionate. He was disappointed that he wasn't going to be able to get another piece of her in the morning before they checked out as he had planned. However, he accepted it for what it was. A fucked-up situation.

They got dressed in silence. Both of them hating the fact that their little rendezvous had come to an abrupt end. When they walked out the hotel it was raining, but luckily they were able to wait under the overhang while the valet got the car. All the while, Wes stood there holding Rayna in his arms.

On the way to her house, Rayna told him all about her sister Alissa and her abusive relationship. She recalled the countless times that she had to be called and told that Alissa was once again in the hospital, behind something her boyfriend had done to her.

Wes wasn't the type of nigga that put his hands on females and didn't respect or like the bitch-ass niggaz that did.

According to Rayna, Alissa's boyfriend cane home drunk as usual. She told Wes that they began arguing when they first arrived at the hotel, then he ended up beating her ass. This time, he supposedly beat her so bad that she thought he would actually kill her. When he stopped beating her ass to take a shit, Alissa snuck out the apartment and ran. Tired, sore, ashamed, and afraid that he would find her, Alissa ran all the way to Rayna's in the rain and was now sitting on her front porch. The distance from Rayna's house to hers was about mile away.

When Wes pulled up in front of Rayna's, he could see a small silhouette crouched down low on her front porch. Neither of them had an umbrella, so together they got wet as he walked Rayna to her front porch where a frightened Alissa waited. It looked like Alissa was sending someone a text message when they approached. She slipped her phone into her pocket as Rayna pulled her up and to her understanding arms.

Wes offered to stay once Rayna got a crying Alissa to calm down. Rayna told him that wasn't necessary because Alissa's boyfriend didn't know where she lived. Against his better judgement, Wes left the two women because he didn't want to come across as too overbearing or thirsty. He and Rayna shared a kiss that held so much promise for the next time. Promises that would never be fulfilled.

Chapter 21

Wes was so engrossed in his conversation with Rayna as he pulled up to her house, that he never took the time to scan her street for any potential dangers. Which was why he never paid any attention to the all-black 2017 Dodge Charger with the limo tints. A costly mistake.

Another reason was because thoughts of all the sexual things Rayna and he had done to one another earlier that night were on constant replay in his mind. They continued to replay so vividly that he could actually taste her and feel the sensations her body caused. He smiled to himself at the fact that he became aroused again just thinking about her. He thought to himself, if she played her cards right, he would consider fucking with her on a serious level.

The all-black Charger trailed the Porsche at a safe distance. Reco was playing it safe, making sure that there was no way they would be spotted. The rain that was now falling in buckets helped with their stealth.

MoMo, in his impatience, kept telling Reco to speed up so they wouldn't lose him. Reco ignored him. He knew what he was doing and didn't need MoMo messing with him, fucking up his concentration. Reco wanted these niggaz just as much as MoMo did. He wasn't going to risk fucking up a good chance like this because he was being too impatient.

T.G. never took his eyes off of the Porsche's taillights. He had the image of them muthafuckas embedded in his mind. Payback was a bitch and he was the hoes' pimp. He gripped his hand around the handle of the gun in his lap, anticipating the kill.

When Reco saw Wes slowing down, getting ready to pull into a driveway, he called it out, "That's got to be it right there." There was no need for him to call it out, though. T.G. and MoMo were already on it. They both sat up in their seats on full alert, ready to go.

Reco quickly pulled over and killed his headlights. They were a little more than half a block away from where Wes pulled into the driveway. The Charger's doors came open right away. The three soon-to-be killers disappeared into the night.

Wes' mind was still on Rayna when he made it home and pulled into his driveway. The time on the screen of his phone read 3:27 am. He thought about calling Rayna, but he didn't want to seem thirsty. Her voice sounded so sweet when she was calling out his name in ecstasy, he just needed to hear it one more time. An idea came to his mind. He would be able to hear her voice and wouldn't seem thirsty, if he called and told her that he was just making sure that she and Alissa were okay. Before he was able to talk himself out of it, Wes found her contact in his phone and pressed the send button. The sound of the raindrops hitting the Porsche was getting louder. Being a true Frisconian, Wes knew that tell-tale sign of a storm coming off of the Pacific Ocean.

He sat and listened while the phone rang on the other end. While he was waiting, he thought he saw movement out of his right peripheral, but when he turned to check it out, nothing was there.

"Hello." She finally answered on the fourth ring, sounding tired.

"Hey, it's me, Wes. I just got home and before I headed in, I wanted to make sure you two were okay. I know you said her boyfriend didn't know where you lived, but I still wanted check in." He was rambling on like a high school kid.

Rayna was smiling brightly on the other end of the phone. She was hoping Wes would call after the night they shared. She couldn't get him off of her mind. Him calling her worried about her safety not only told her that he was a good man, it also told her that she was more than just a fuck. The average nigga would not have given a fuck enough to call and make sure she was safe.

"Oh, hello, Wes." To him, it sounded like her voice perked up. "Thanks for calling. That's so nice of you. We're okay. I

144

got her to take a hot shower after sitting outside in the cold rain for so long. She couldn't stop shivering. After her shower I laid down with her and she fell right to sleep. I was just laying down trying to go to sleep myself. But I kept wondering if you were going to call. I didn't want to miss you if you did." She couldn't believe she actually told him the truth.

"So, you must be really checking for a nigga if you were fighting your sleep, hoping I was going to call?" There it was again. This time, though, the movement was out his left peripheral vision.

"So, what if I am? Is that a bad thing?" Wes never heard the question. At the same exact time he turned his head to the left, lightning flashed, illuminating the night sky. It was like a scene out of a *Wes Craven's Nightmare*. When the lightning lit up the night sky, Wes saw three hooded figures standing outside of his window with grimaces on their faces. They resembled three Grim Reapers.

He dropped the cell phone and reached down under his seat for his gun. It was a good attempt, but a futile one, nevertheless.

Reco stood in the middle of the trio. When he saw the recollected fear register in Wes' eyes, he grinned and pulled the trigger. Muzzle flashes licked the tip of the barrel of the .45 a fraction of a second before the sound of the big gun erupted. MoMo's own mini missile was only a decimal of a second behind Reco's. T.G.'s was right behind. Together, one after the other, a barrage of mini missiles in the form of bullets executed their mission and found their target.

The copper bullets tore into the door and window of the Porsche, shattering the glass as they proceeded to barrel into Wes' face, skull, and body. The three stood tall and firm in the dark, resembling the cowboys of the Wild Wild West. The three thunderous guns going off simultaneously silenced the loud thunder.

They all continued to squeeze their triggers until their guns were empty. When they were done, they didn't bother running. They simply walked back down the street under the guise of rain, back to the Charger.

Rayna blinked her eyes, stunned. She knew the sound of a gunshot just about as clear as she knew the sound of a car's horn. She was born and raised in Sunnydale. She had been around gunshots her entire life.

"Wes, what's going on?" Fear clutched her chest when he didn't answer her.

On her end of the phone, it sounded like Wes was in the middle of a shootout. The problem with that was he was in the middle of a conversation with her when the shooting began. Which meant he wasn't prepared for or ready to be in no damn shootout. To Rayna, this could only mean one thing, he was a victim.

"Wes! Wes!" This time she screamed into the phone as if he would be able to hear her over the loud gunshots. "Wes, please… Answer me, got damnit!" she screamed hysterically. Deep in the crevices of her heart, Rayna knew the truth. Her mind didn't want to let her accept the cold reality. Still, she knew. She could feel it. Wes had just been murdered while on the phone talking to her. All kinds of emotions went through her mind. She and Wes had only been talking for a few weeks, but she really liked him. Sleeping with him tonight was her opening the door and letting him into her life. She wasn't some hoe or neighborhood bopper. She didn't just go sleeping around with niggaz. Just because she worked at a strip club didn't mean she was a hoe. She really liked him, she thought to herself again, realizing this time that she had just been robbed of the opportunity to get to know him better. Robbed of a chance to possibly pursue a shot at happiness with him. The two of them could've had a beautiful future together, but it was stolen. Like so many other beautiful dreams in this fucked up city!

Rayna didn't even realize she was crying. The tears rolled down her pretty face as she still held the phone to her ear. Listening to nothing. Her young heart slowly breaking into a million tiny little feelings. She was thinking how much she hated the dreadful fucking city of San Francisco. For the first time in her young life, she thought about leaving the city. She had, had enough of its ugly violence. Enough of its tragedies. Enough of its let downs.

If Rayna wasn't so engrossed in her sorrow or trying to concentrate so hard on hearing some kind of sound on the other end of the phone, looking for any sort of proof or glimmer of hope that she was wrong, she would have heard Alissa when she came walking down the hallway. If Rayna would have turned around, she would have been shocked to see a look of happiness on her best friend's face. Had Rayna gotten up from her living room couch at that moment and walked into her back room, she would have walked in on Alissa sending a happy face emoji to Reco's cell phone.

Chapter 22

5:12 am

C1ty woke up early this morning. G-Baby was doing good on her recovery, and he wanted to take her away from the city for a while to get her mind off things. He made reservations for the two of them to stay the week at the Hilton in Monterey. She could finish the rest of her healing and relaxation along the coastline. He hoped it would do some good to keep her mind off the stress that the news he gave her may have caused.

While taking a shower, he made a mental note to go to Access Corrections and send some money before he took off. J was C1ty's big brother from another mother. They met in 4-J-West when C1ty did a year in County for his third DUI, while J was doing a life sentence. J took a liking to a young C1ty, who had a good head on his shoulders and was always thirsty for knowledge, of which J was a water well of information. He and C1ty would talk as often as they could on a vast variety of subjects.

C1ty respected J for the way he carried himself and the fact that he would take the time to drop jewels and teach the youngsters in the Pod. The main youngster being C1ty. When C1ty got out, the two of them stayed in contact. The wealth of knowledge continued to come and C1ty, in return, made sure he looked out and dropped some bread on J's books for commissary.

He was in the middle of his third rinse when G-Baby walked in the bathroom and told him that he had a phone call. He heard the tears she cried in her voice. He opened the shower door with a look of concern on his face.

"Baby, why you crying? What's wrong? Who is it?" He fired the questions off with rapid-fire concern. It had to be someone calling with some seriously fucked up news if G-Baby was crying.

"Just take the phone, De'Mario. Please, I can't tell." That fucked him up even more.

He reached out and took the cell phone. G-Baby sat down on the toilet, put her head in her hands, and openly cried. C1ty braced himself for what he was about to hear.

"Hello?"

He listened to the voice on the other end of the line. Silently, he said a prayer, begging God not to let the information be true. His tears blended in with the water that was already running down his face. He tried to speak, but the lump in his throat wouldn't allow him to. His knees buckled. They wanted to give out on him, but he wouldn't let them.

He dropped the cell phone. It hit the porcelain tub, cracking the touch screen, the water completely destroying it. C1ty paid it no attention. He didn't even take time to console G-Baby as he bolted out of the shower. He was numb. No thoughts. No sounds. No feelings.

He rushed to put some clothes on and bolted out of the front door with his Glock in his hand. It was still raining outside. That didn't stop him from pushing the Camaro to dangerously high speeds as he raced to his little brother's house. The tears didn't fall, they poured down his face.

The fact that there were casualties in every war wasn't foreign to C1ty. They all knew that the Reaper could come for any one of them at any moment. The only question on his heart was, why Wes? Out of all the members involved, why did Wes have to be the fucking casualty!

He almost lost control of the Camaro when he hit Wes's block. The Camaro fishtailed violently like an angry metal shark pursuing its prey. He could see police lights in the distance. As he regained control of the car and raced down the street, he could make out a large crowd of bystanders, police cars, and a city van.

"Nosey muthafuckas!" he shouted in reference to the crowd of nosey bystanders.

The Camaro hit a puddle of water and hydroplaned. Again, C1ty lost control. He came within inches of side swiping a black Dodge Charger that was parked next to the curb. Once again, he regained control of the car.

By this time, all eyes were on the vehicle speeding recklessly down the street toward them. Even the police officers' attention was drawn to the car speeding down the street.

When C1ty slammed on his brakes, the tires skidded across the pavement, sending up a massive cloud of smoke. The loud screech of the tires could be heard blocks away.

As soon as the Camaro came to a complete stop, C1ty jumped out looking like the ambassador to the Devil himself. He paid no one any attention. C1ty's eyes were focused on his brother's truck. Yellow caution tape was everywhere. The entire sidewalk from the neighbor's property on one side of Wes's house to the neighbor's house on the other side was blocked off with yellow tape. Several officers were spread out through the crowd looking for anyone who would possibly make a statement, while a couple of officers did crowd control.

A young white rookie with not even a month on the force stood directly in C1ty's path. The rookie officer knew he couldn't show the fear that was in his heart. He knew he had to be assertive and show authority. Which was why, as C1ty got within feet of the tape, the rookie officer took one step forward and put his hand out to stop C1ty. This gesture placed the officer's hand directly in the center of C1ty's chest.

"I'm sorry, Sir, but I am not going to be allowed to permit you past this caution tape." He was trying to reason with a raging bull.

C1ty quickly grabbed the officer's arm, snatched him close to his chest, and spun him around so quick. The rookie didn't know what happened. Still keeping the movement going, he shoved the officer out of his way.

"You better keep your fucking hands off of me!" C1ty demanded as he ducked under the tape.

Several officers rushed to the officer's aid as he stumbled forward, desperately trying to gain his balance. Seeing the disaster that was about to take place, Don and Dell, who happened to be standing on the sidewalk talking to a sergeant, rushed to intervene.

"Wait! Wait! That's our brother!" they both yelled, almost in unison.

A brief pushing and shoving match ensued. Officers yelled orders, which C1ty ignored. Dell and Don yelled at the officers, who were pulling on an outraged C1ty. It was brief chaos until the same sergeant who Dell and Don were talking to came to break it up and bring about order. Only because he heard the two brothers yell the young man was their brother.

"I wanna see my brother." C1ty sounded more like a hurt, scared child than a goon from the streets.

"Son, we're sorry, but that isn't going to be possible. The city coroner—"

"Bitch ass nigga! I don't give a fuck about the city coroner! I need to see my little brother." His pain pulled at the heart of the onlookers.

"I'm sorry, Sir, but this is a homicide investigation—" This time the officer was cut off by the sergeant, who felt he needed to de-escalate the situation.

"Sir, I'm terribly sorry for your loss—"

C1ty didn't even let him get started. "Nigga, you ain't sorry! But I promise you, yo' ass gone be sorry if I can't see my muthafuck'n brother!" The threat was heard by all.

The 6'2", 220-pound sergeant didn't like the shitty attitude of the skinny punk kid in front of him. More importantly, he wasn't going to allow anyone to talk to him the way the kid did in front of his men. He was sympathetic to the kid's loss, but enough was enough.

"Like it or not, son, you're not going to be able to see the deceased. This is a crime scene—"

"Yeah, alright!" C1ty turned around while the Sergeant was still talking.

The crowd parted like the Red Sea as he stormed back to his Camaro. Dell was the eldest brother. He knew his brother too well to just stand by and do nothing, knowing damn well what C1ty was about to do. Dell rushed and caught up with C1ty.

"Mario, think about what you're about to do. It's three of us against more than ten cops in front of only God knows how many witnesses." Dell had run in front of him, blocking his path.

"Dell, get the fuck out my way!"

"Nigga, what do you think you're about to do?" Dell could clearly see the hurt on his little brother's face.

"Them bitch ass pigs 'bout to let me see him, Dell. I need to see him, my nigga!" C1ty shouted. His face was so wet from tears the moonlight shone off of it.

"I know, lil' brah. But if you grab that banger, you still not gone see him. We either gone be next to him or we gone be in jail headed for prison."

"I don't give a fuck 'bout none of that! Dell, he was my little brother. Them bitch ass niggaz stole my little brother from me!" C1ty was ready to murder somebody, any-fucking-body!

Dell reached out with both arms and took his little brother in his arms. C1ty broke down like a five-year-old who just lost his parents.

Dell felt like shit. He was the oldest. It was his job to protect all of them, and he failed. His baby brother was less than fifteen feet away from him. Dead at the tender age of twenty. Dead before his life even got started.

Dell whispered into C1ty's ear, "My nigga, we gotta think straight and move mean. I want the streets to drink the blood of every last one of them bitch ass Sunnydale niggaz! Nigga, that's on the Mobb!"

C1ty heard Dell, but all he could think about at the time was his little brother being dead. At that moment, nothing mattered. Not G-Baby, the police, revenge, jail, death, nothing!

It was over another hour or so before the last of the police officers drove off from the house. By this time, the rain had let up and the morning sun was rising. CJ, XO, and Murda had all shown up by this time as well. The five relatives had just walked into Wes's house so they could all talk and try to make heads and tails of what happened.

The all-black Dodge Charger finally pulled away from the curb. Reco, MoMo, and T.G. had never left. After killing Wes, MoMo came up with the idea not to leave. They instead sat behind the tinted windows and watched the entire scene play out in front of them.

The Charger came to a stop in the middle of the street in front of the house. The front and back passenger side windows came down. T.G. and MoMo both hung their arms with guns ready out of the windows and opened fire.

CJ was the first to respond to the sound of the gunshots. He dove, tackling C1ty, who was standing in front of the window. If it wasn't for CJ's quick reflexes. C1ty would have been killed by the two bullets that flew by exactly where his head was at moments ago. Everyone else recovered quickly and began returning fire.

The shootout was very brief. The exchange of gunfire only lasted a few seconds. XO flung the front door open just as the Charger was pulling off. He squeezed the trigger, relentlessly sending shots at the vehicle as it sped away. Murda and C1ty were fast on XO's heels. They all sent shots at the Charger to no avail. It turned the corner and sped away. That's when C1ty realized that was the same Charger he had almost side swiped when he raced down the street a little over an hour ago.

Right on cue, thunder lit up the sky and the rain began to fall again.

Chapter 23

"The recent surge in gun violence that has gripped our city is unbelievably heartbreaking and outright shameful. It pains my heart as not only the mayor but as a fellow born and raised San Franciscan. The recent wave in gang activity that has wrecked our community is not only destroying our city, but it's adding to the eradication of our people from this country. People, I am not only speaking to you as your mayor. I am appealing to you as a black woman."

Mayor Breed's emotions could be felt to all in attendance at the Mayor Willie Brown Youth Center in the heart of Sunnydale. "A black woman who can remember growing up as a kid in the projects of Hunters Point before moving to the Filmore District. I remember being terrified hearing the many gunshots at night from the countless shootouts. I remember vividly the many sorrow-filled faces on the families of murder victims at funerals. The daily candlelight vigils. I cannot forget nor escape the trauma of growing up in these conditions.

"Sadly, I can also remember the countless politicians who made so many empty bureaucratic speeches and promises about what they were going to do to clean up our community. The campaigns they all ran on cleaning up our city streets. Please, I implore you to listen to me. The police and other law enforcement can't solve our problem. Outside agencies can't solve our problem. White suburbia cannot solve our problem. Only we can! We must solve the conflicts and grudges that our children hold against one another that are causing the violence. We must get to the heart of the problem that caused the hatred that they possess for one another. It is our job as mothers, fathers, aunts, and uncles, teachers, and community leaders. It is up to us as a people to care enough to then step up and become a part of the solution!" Her powerful words continued. Her heartfelt speech continued, but Rick had heard enough.

Rick knew all too well what the mayor was talking about. He knew the tragic pain and heartache that she spoke of. He knew it intimately.

Rick looked at the photo in his shaky hand. He kept the photo with him everywhere that he went. Often looking at it fifty, sometimes seventy-five times a day. This photo meant more to him than anything in the world. To him, it was more than just a photo. It was the reason for everything.

"Don't worry, my sistah, you are not alone. I promise. In due time." He was speaking to Mayor Breed, but he mumbled it to himself.

Rick stood up from his seat at the back of the Rec Center. He looked at the mayor one last time, and then he walked out. Outside, the midday sky was gloomy and overcast. Remnants of the three-day storm that just passed was evident in the large formations of water along the street. The formations were too big to be considered puddles. In the parking lot of the Youth Center, there was a body of water that spanned the entire width of the parking lot and was nearly a foot-and-a-half deep.

A sense of nostalgia overcame Rick as he recalled memories of years ago, long before the name was changed to the Mayor Willie Brown Youth Center. Over thirty-plus years ago, when it was simply known as "The Rec." That day would forever be embedded in his heart. Today, though, he couldn't afford to let the memory of that day invade his mind. He blinked his eyes and shook his head side to side, erasing the memory for the time being.

Making sure to avoid the water on the ground so he wouldn't fuck up his shoes, Rick made his way over to the Mediterranean blue Maybach that was parked at the curb in front of the Boys and Girls Club next door. The moment his driver knew Rick was comfortable, she pulled away from the curb.

A little later, the Maybach pulled into the parking lot of Hard-Knox, a soul food restaurant on 3rd and Filmore Street. Rick was busy reading e-mails and handling other business.

He was a very busy man, and his time was important. Not long after they pulled into the parking lot, his driver lowered the partition.

"He's making his way over here now, Sir," she informed Rick.

"Okay, Honey. Thank you." He raised the partition. Rick put his work away and prepared for his guest.

When the young man reached the Maybach, the doors were unlocked and Rick lowered the back passenger window.

"Climb in," Rick called out of the open window.

Rick could tell right away that the young Samoan wasn't happy. He had a look on his face of an angry man ashamed of his actions. Rick reasoned that guilt would eat a muthafucka up every time. That was MoMo's problem, not Rick's. the young nigga would just have to live with the consequences of his actions.

"You had me thinking for a moment that maybe you didn't want your money," Rick told MoMo once he closed the door.

"I'm always gone check my children, OG That's why this shit is Tear It Off." MoMo had to let the old nigga know so he wouldn't get shit fucked up.

Rick didn't take the youngsta's demeanor nor attitude to heart. He knew the kid was feeling bad about the blood money he was about to receive.

"You could've fooled me. I'm not a man accustomed to calling people more than once. Especially when I'm trying to pay them for services rendered."

"Yeah, well. Maybe you ain't noticed, but we've been real busy. That shit you asked me to do started a war."

"So, I've heard. That's why I doubled the agreed upon price, figured more money is something you could always use in a war. I didn't realize you and your friends would take things so far. But, anyway, hopefully the extra money will be of use to you." Rick didn't give a fuck about MoMo or any other member of the Tear It Off Clique.

His plan had worked out beautifully. A couple of months prior, Rick offered MoMo ten thousand dollars to embarrass C1ty in front of G-Baby. This was why MoMo fucked with G-Baby at the show that night. It was all a part of an elaborate plan by Rick to start a war between the two hoods. Things could not have gone any better than they did.

Rick handed MoMo a large manilla envelope that contained twenty thousand dollars. MoMo thought about Bubz and his mom, and A-Wax and Creep-Thru. All of their blood was on his hands. They died behind this deal with the OG.

All of a sudden, MoMo didn't want to be around the old slick muthafucka no more. He grabbed the envelope with the money and got out of the car without saying another word.

When MoMo left, Rick let out a booming laugh. Everything was working out beautifully. In fact, things were going so good with the first part of his plans that he decided he would initiate the second part early. Phase two was sure to get things rocking and rolling without any doubt. He pushed a button on the arm rest of the door, signaling to the driver that it was time to go. Then, on second thought, he buzzed the intercom.

"You know what, since we're already here, I think we should drop in and get something to eat."

"Okay, Uncle. That sounds great."

Rick didn't wait for her to get out and open his door. He did it himself, and together, they walked inside of the restaurant as the rain began to fall again.

***

Like most of the fucked-up things in life, shit only ran downhill. At least that's how Sgt. M. Dudley felt. First, some pen-pushing bureaucrat got wind of a few killings and alerted the governor, who always wanted people to think that he was doing his job. So, he got ahold of the mayor, who then contacted the police chief, and so on and so forth. Until some enormous, big-nose, badly balding, freckle-faced, fat fuck who looked like he was one hot dog away from a heart attack, and happened to be the captain, brought his fat ass into Dudley's office, yelling and talking out of his ass about shit he knew nothing about. Making all kinds of empty threats.

Sgt. Dudley, a veteran sergeant, happened to be in charge of the Bayview Police Department's Gang Task Force Division that covered the area known as the Ingleside District. The district included the gangs from Bayview Hunter Point, Visitacion Valley, Excelsior, and Portola. The area's main gangs were Tre-4, Tear It Off, The Low, D.B.G. Tower Side Gang, Lake View, Alemany, E-Mobb, and, of course, Excelsior.

His department was undermanned and overworked. He and his boys worked hard and kicked ass. They took pride in their job and didn't need any of the above bureaucrat brass assholes all in their shit, fucking with him or his people.

The entire time Captain Sweeney was on his tirade, Sgt. Dudley just stared at the little man, wondering what it would feel like to pull his 9mm from its holster and put a bullet right smack in the middle of the Captain's reddish forehead. He could literally see his fat black head snap backward from the force of the bullet before the back of his cranium exploded. Sending greyish and pink brain matter and skull fragments all over the office door.

Even after the captain left, Sgt. Dudley allowed the sadistic fantasy to continue to play out inside of his mind. Receiving some kind of sick euphoria from the brutal, twisted fantasy.

Sgt. Dudley didn't need Captain Sweeney nor anybody else giving him a so-called crash course on the gangs in his district in the form of a lecture. He was well aware of what was happening, knew all about the war between Sunnydale and Double Rock, or, to be more precise, the war between Tear It Off and The 357 Mobb. The shooting up of the funeral at the church was a brazen display of disrespect, but it still wasn't the talk of the town. That reward went to the crazy sons of bitches that killed the Double Rock kid, then had the balls to stay on the scene and watch everything until the police left. Only to do a drive-by and shoot up the exact same house.

He ran his hand through his shoulder-length, wavy, brown hair. Sgt. Dudley was both shocked and impressed by the audacity of the young kids nowadays. They didn't give two shits about respect unless they were telling you that you needed to respect them. Little nappy-headed crumb snatchers crying about and trying to demand something that was alien to them to begin with.

He reached for his mug of the nasty shit water that passed for coffee at the precinct. Nicknamed shit water because it looked and tasted like something out of the depths of New York city's corroded sewage system. The dark motor oil look-a-like did the job. It was the kind of shit that would wake the dead and put hair on their chest. After 74 hours straight, it was just what the doctor ordered.

It was the sergeant's third and final cup of the morning. That and a couple of day-old, stale donuts would serve as breakfast. Later, maybe he'd eat a real breakfast. Right now, he had work to do. So, this would have to suffice.

After downing the last of the shit water, he noticed the sour taste and rancid smell of his own breath. Drinking three cups of shit water, after going three days without brushing his teeth, had the sergeant's breath smelling like a Taiwanese hooker's ass after working in a Bangkok whore house all night. Oh well, it was just another lovely perk of the job.

He sat the coffee mug back down on his desk and got up to leave. It was time to hit the pavement. Sgt. Dudley had work to do. It was time to kick some ass and take some names.

Chapter 24

"Yeah, that's my bad, homie. You know we wasn't expecting that shit to go down like that with the homie and all. The big homie told me to tell you he sends his sincerest apology, fool. He told me to tell you there's a little something extra in there for your troubles." Fat Boy slow stroked Juanita from behind while he listened to Blinky explain himself like a little bitch on the plane.

He didn't give a fuck about any of the excuses Blinky was giving him. The only fucking thing Fat Boy wanted to know was where in the fuck was his dope. He didn't play no games when it came to his money. If he had to, he would teach Crazy, Hector, and all the rest of the San Francisco muthafuckas about that MMN shit.

The city of East Palo Alto was like a small sovereign state that stood alone directly in the center of a county. Its natives were a breed of genetics unlike any other. No matter the race, its niggaz were different from other niggaz. It's USOs different from other USOs, so on and so forth. Its native Mexicans were different. They didn't look, talk, nor behave like Mexicans anywhere else. Fat Boy didn't give a fuck about a no red-on-red policy. Like everybody else from East Palo Alto and Menlo Park, he followed the Anybody Could Get It Code! ABCG.

Juanita was doing all she could not to call out. She knew Fat Boy would kick her ass if she violated his sale. So, she kept her head buried in the pillow and took the dick. It was some damn good dick. She had already come twice and felt another orgasm coming. For Fat Boy to go from beating the pussy up to long dicking her slowly was sweet, sweet torture. One that she loved.

"Look, rogue, all I know is the shit better be where it's supposed to be, and it better be on point. If my nigga tells me shit ain't right or he had any problems, then all of you gone have problems. Straight up! But if shit is good, then we good." Fat Boy didn't too much like Frisco niggaz anyway because deep down, Frisco niggaz didn't like PA niggas. Hell, nobody really did.

He watched as his dick slid in and out of Juanita. The contrast of her cinnamon-mocha skin swallowing his light-brown skin was a sight for sore eyes. He felt her walls spasming and watched a milky coat cover his dick as her pussy exploded again.

On the other end of the phone, Blinky was ready to blow a head gasket. He didn't know who in the fuck this fat bitch thought he was talking to. Big homie or not, Blinky would cut his fucking balls off and feed them to him. He had to bite his lower lip and slowly count to ten before he went the fuck off. Crazy wouldn't be pleased if Blinky started a war with the arrogant fat fuck.

"Check this out, homie. Everything is everything, like I said. So, your lil' homie ain't gone have no problems. But ain't no putas (bitches) over this way. So, you can send them threats to somebody else, 'cause they don't phase me." He wasn't disrespectful, but he had to let the fool know what time it was with him.

Blinky knew the MMN crew were animals, but he was a fucking beast too!

Fat Boy started to bite on that bullshit hook Blinky threw out there. Right when he got ready to open his mouth, Juanita got to doing that shit with her pussy muscles. They constricted then relaxed around his dick. It felt like she was sucking his dick with her pussy.

"Yeah, we'll see, nigga!" was all Fat Boy could get out.

He ended the call then tossed the phone. Juanita was a super sexy black and Mexican chick. She had a beautiful body and fucked like a Mexican whore. The bitch thought she was funny playing them games with her pussy. He grabbed her by her small waist and started fucking the shit out of her.

Juanita howled like a banshee while he tore that pussy up, her brown ass cheeks clapping their approval.

"Hey, Face!" Fat Boy shouted.

A few seconds later, the door to the room opened and Fat Boy's right-hand man, Scarface, stuck his head in the door.

"What's up, fool?" Juanita's big titties bouncing back and forth, now that Fat Boy was pulling her hair, had Scarface's dick instantly hard.

"Take two of the homies wit' you and go take care of that," Fat Boy ordered. "If it's a problem, fool, let me know right away!"

He never even looked up at Scarface. Fat Boy's eyes were glued on his dick as more and more of the milky white juice covered his shit and ran down her legs.

"You already know, fool!" Scarface responded.

"You already know." Fat Boy couldn't hold back anymore.

He smacked her hard on her big ass and pounded his way home while that ass jiggled. Just before he bust his nutt, he smiled, hoping something went wrong.

***

After parking the Toyota Camry in the parking lot of the Tom Fran Mall, Trucho walked back over to Chino, who was waiting inside of his Impala. It was parked a couple of rows behind the Toyota, clearly in their view.

"Trust me on this, little brother. Everything is going to work out as planned, you'll see. Pretty soon, all of this shit is going to be over. Once I'm the big homie, we gone take over the entire Mission, fool. We're gonna be richer than anything you could ever imagine. You gotta trust me, Trucho."

Trucho paid close attention to what his brother was saying, but he found it hard to believe that the committee of big homies would just openly agree to give Chino their blessing to sell other drugs just because he took over for Crazy. That was if he would be able to pull off his little takeover to begin with. It was a hell of a gamble. One that would surely cost them their lives if they didn't succeed. Still, he trusted his older brother. Chino had always led Trucho in the right direction.

They made everybody think that there was animosity between the two of them, but it was just a part of Chino's plan. He figured if the homies thought Trucho was jealous or envious of Chino, then they would openly share their hidden displeasure they had in their own hearts. Chino knew that some people would have larceny in their hearts. He wanted to spot the snakes as early as he possibly could.

"I'm with you, Chino, you know that. I don't care what it takes, whatever we have to do, I'm with it because I'm with you."

"We're going to make our move real soon, Trucho. Everything is falling in place. We just got to align a few more things in order to make sure we got it all right. You just be ready." As Chino was talking, he watched as a black Infinity pulled into the parking lot and parked next to the Toyota.

They watched as the back door of the Infinity opened. A younger homie, no doubt a soldier, hopped out of the Infinity and made his way over to the unlocked Toyota and climbed in. Moments later, the Toyota pulled out and drove off. The Infinity pulled out of the parking lot behind the Toyota.

Chino waited a few more minutes before pulling out of the parking lot himself.

Everything was ready. It was time for Chino to take some pieces off this chess board he had been setting up nicely. Trucho, Smokey, and Casper were his handpicked, carefully chosen compadres. They were the three he thought he could trust. Therefore, they were the three he conspired with. It was time to see if they had what it took. El Negro reached out to Chino last night. It was time, El Negro told him, for Chino to handle his business. This was the call that Chino had been waiting on.

God damn right, it was time. Chino took his cell phone out his pocket and made a call.

"It's all you, homeboy," he told the person on the other end of the line when they picked up.

There was no response from the other end of the line. Chino didn't expect one. Everything that needed to be said was already said. He made a left turn at the light and jumped on the freeway. A storm was coming. It was time to go pay Blinky a visit. Chino needed to check in for active duty!

***

"Alright, niggaz, it's simple. Them bitch ass MMN muthafuckas got it, I want it, and we need it." The deep voice sounded like the voice of God as it crackled over the four-way walkie talkies. "We gone hit these muthafuckas hard and fast, so let's make it good! I don't want them to make it to the freeway, so we gone hit they ass at this traffic light!" Responses came immediately over the walkie talkies.

When Scarface chose to take lil' Snoopy with him on the pick-up, Snoopy felt that this was going to be the opportunity he had been waiting on to step up to the plate and show the homies that he was ready to take a more active role in the gang. At sixteen years of age, Snoopy was tired of being one of the smallest men on the totem pole. He was tired of everyone looking at him like he was a nobody. He wanted muthafuckas to put some respect on his name, like that one rapper, Bird Man.

He pulled up to the stoplight. Thoughts of him becoming the next American Gangster came to a sudden halt at the sound of tires screeching loudly when a van came to a sudden stop in front of the car Snoop was driving. It would've been the perfect time to put all his thoughts of making a name for himself to use. Unfortunately for Snoop, that didn't happen. All of his previous thoughts about becoming a gangsta quickly evaporated. His mind came up blank as he froze up out of shock and fear.

Suddenly, another car pulled in behind Snoop, who sat and watched as doors came open and niggas hopped out holding Choppas.

"Y'all know what time it is, nigga, Tear It Off!" Butch tried his best to impersonate the members of the Tear It Off Clique. He himself was E-Mobb, but he needed the Mexicans to think the TIO were the ones to rob them.

That was the deal he had with Chino. Chino was allowing Butch to keep all of the meth, as long as Butch made Scarface and Fat Boy think TIO was behind the robbery. This would cause conflict between the two gangs, and Butch didn't have any problem with that. Especially if it meant he could keep all of the dope for him and his niggaz.

Scarface knew he had to think fast. The lil' homies would no doubt look to him for leadership. They would follow his lead. The problem with that was, Scarface was ready to piss his pants himself.

"Nigga, we don't know what the fuck y'all talking 'bout!" Scarface figured he would play tough.

Lil' Zeke used the butt of the shotgun he held in his hands and cracked Scarface across the side of his head through the passenger window, which was rolled down.

That was the moment Chewy decided he wasn't going out like no little bitch. From the backseat, Chewy upped his Glock .23 and sent two wild shots in Lil' Zeke's direction. The first went over Lil' Zeke's head. The second caught him in the shoulder.

Before Scarface could react to the two bullets that just flew by his head, the backseat of the car they were in was filled with an army of bullets. Chewy was killed instantly.

"Alright! Alright!" Scarface was scared out of his mind. "It's in the back on the floor!" He gave up the info like a five-dollar trick giving up the body.

"Check it out!" Butch ordered.

"Bingo!" Lil' Zeke yelled, pulling the duffel bag that was on the floor out of the car.

Scarface knew he had fucked up by giving up the meth. But the only thing that mattered at that moment was him keeping his life. He wasn't ready to go meet his brother in the afterlife.

After getting what they had come for, Butch and his crew hopped back inside their vehicles and disappeared. Scarface knew there would be hell to pay once Fat Boy found out what happened. He could only pray that it wasn't him who was going to have to pay.

He and Snoop bounced out of the car as soon as Butch and them took off. They ran until they found the security and shelter of some apartment complexes. There, Scarface pulled out his cellphone and called Fat Boy.

"Hello?" Fat Boy answered. He was watching a porno while Juanita had her mouth filled with his dick.

"Fat Boy, we got a problem." Those were the last words that the young boss wanted to hear. I need you to have somebody pick me and Snoop up."

"What? Where the fuck you at, nigga?" Fat Boy pushed Juanita's head out of his lap. He was ready to kill somebody.

Fat Boy knew that if there was a problem, it meant somebody fucked with his shit, and he wasn't about to have that! Nobody fucked with Fat Boy!

Nobody!

Chapter 25

The 5'2", slim Mexican female walked out of Two Jack's with her food in her little arms, thanking God that she was going to make it back before the rain came again.

Her name was Alissa. Though she wasn't part of TIO, she was from the Tre-4 and fucked with the clique as much as any bitch from the hood. In fact, out of all the little broads in the hood, Alissa was Auntie Dee's favorite. The fellas couldn't see Alissa in the same light as the rest of the broads because she was not only ugly, but she had the body of a ten-year-old boy. Who the fuck could get aroused from that? Since she couldn't sleep her way up the ladder of importance, Alissa secured her position by running errands and doing favors for the clique, like she did today. Running to Two Jack's to get some food for everybody.

When she saw the 5'11", 205-pound, dark-skinned nigga with the fresh taper and perfectly lined beard, Alissa stumbled over one of the many cracks in the ground. She was too busy watching CJ instead of paying attention to where she was going.

"Easy, Lil' Momma, I gotcha," he told her as his strong arms wrapped around her petite little body.

Alissa could feel the muscles in his arms as he held on to her. She was instantly attracted. CJ helped her stand straight up on her own two feet.

"Thank you. I'm so embarrassed. Had you not been there to catch me, I surely would've busted my shit." She avoided eye contact to mask her embarrassment.

"Hell, if I hadn't been there to distract you in the first place, I don't think you would've tripped." The way he looked at her and bit his bottom lip made her lower regions moist.

After nearly fifteen minutes of conversation, Alissa realized the fellas were going to kill her. Not only was she late, but the food had already gone cold. When she addressed her concerns to CJ, he not only offered to replace the food, but he also told her that he would give her a ride back. This would give them time to get to know one another some more. This excited Alissa. She had never had a man as fine as CJ show an interest in her.

Alissa had no clue as to how many days ago it was that she met the handsome man, who turned out to be the Devil, at Two Jack's. She never made it back to Auntie Dee's where the fellas waited. CJ did give her a ride. He sprayed a mist in her face that knocked her out. When Alissa woke up, she was cold, completely naked, and every one of her holes was sore. The pain added with the sticky substance between her legs told her that she had been raped.

The real nightmare began when she woke up. CJ came into the room where she was naked and tied up, lying on a mattress on the floor. A giant of a man, whom CJ referred to as X, joined him. They took turns raping and beating Alissa until she answered every single last question they asked her about Tear It Off.

At least all the questions she could answer.

***

The thick gash over Blinky's eyebrow bled profusely. He had to continue blinking to avoid getting blood into his eye. His hands were zip tied. His thigh hurt like fuck from the bullet that was buried inside of it. A dirty sock was rammed in his mouth, held in place by duct tape. He was on the floor of his living room watching helplessly while Jessica was bent over getting fucked from behind by Chino while she sucked Trucho's dick at the same time. From her moans of pleasure, Blinky could tell she was having the time of her life.

They had come in while Blinky was in the shower. He walked naked out of the shower to the living room to find out why his bitch was ignoring him. He got the surprise of his lifetime as he walked in on her sitting on the couch with one hand between her legs playing with her pussy, while Chino stood in front of her with his dick down her throat.

Chino had his gun trained steadily on a fuming Blinky. He would've taken his chances with Chino had it not been for Trucho. He sat at the dining room table with his gun trained on Blinky too.

While Jessica sucked his dick, Chino told Blinky about the new regime and the vision he had for 21st Street. There was no room in the new regime for Crazy or anybody loyal to him. Blinky understood he was a dead man anyway. So, he took his chances. He openly charged Chino, just wanting to get his hands around the traitorous bastard's throat. Chino wasted no time shooting Blinky in his right thigh. The bullet caused the big man to tumble forward.

A few blows to the head from the barrel of the gun in Chino's hand made sure Blinky stayed down. Trucho tied Blinky up, and Chino told the killer all about his first meeting with Jessica. How he'd fucked her from behind while she was bent over the couch. And how she loved it when he forced his dick deep inside her asshole. Blinky was furious. He couldn't do anything about the disrespect he was receiving at the hands of his own little homies.

After swallowing all of Trucho's nutt, Jessica craned her head back and moaned loudly as Chino fucked the life out of her pussy. She couldn't help herself. The sight of the notorious Blinky helplessly bleeding on the floor like a bitch while Chino the real Alpha male screwed her recklessly in front of him was a pleasure like none other to her. It was like her mind was off of two quadruple stacks of ecstasy and two Mollys at the same time she was getting gang fucked by her own gang.

Her eyes of passion were only silenced when Casper took Trucho's placed and shoved his dick in her eagerly waiting mouth. The fuck session lasted hours, until every last man had his fill. With the blood of Blinky and the pussy juices of

Jessica on their dicks. Smokey, Casper, and Trucho pledged their loyalty and alliance to Chino.

Chino pulled out of knife and told Jessica to show her loyalty and pledge her alliance, she had to kill Blinky. She was a bout it bitch from day one. She didn't hesitate to take the knife from Chino and stab Blinky over ten times when she was done. Chino had her drop the knife into a Ziploc bag he had. Just as a little added insurance. After going over the story she was supposed to give the police, Chino tied her up and pistol whipped her before they all walked out. The police would find the two of them three days later. Blinky's sister, who came over looking to borrow some money, would discover both Blinky and Jessica's bodies lying tied up on the floor of the living room.

Chapter 26

Murda and XO sat as still as corpses in the blackness of the night. They melted invisibly into the shadows of the night, waiting on their victim. Wes' funeral was in the morning, and they both felt that they needed to do this in honor of their dead cousin. Their fallen comrade.

When they first saw the thirty-something-year-old Hispanic-looking woman with the big tits come out the door, they each silently wondered if she was the woman they had been waiting for. She fit the description. Thirty-something, 5'7" to 5'9" tall, big tits, and no ass. Dressed in sweatpants and a t-shirt. Once she lit her Newport and started smoking, Murda nudged his brother, letting him know that she was indeed the right person.

As Auntie Dee smoked her Newport, she thought about her nephews and the shit they were in. Usually, Auntie Dee stayed in her lane and out of their business. But, lately, she was beginning to think she should have a talk with them. The incident at Bubz's funeral and what happened to his mother gripped her heart like a pair of vice grips. Auntie Dee didn't want anything else to happen to one of her nephews or any more of their little friends.

It was time, Auntie Dee figured, to tell them all the truth. She had to sit her nephews down and let them know the real before it was too late. She decided that the moment the boys got back, she would tell them everything. Auntie Dee crushed the remainder of her cigarette under her foot and headed back inside her apartment.

The moment Murda saw her stomping the cigarette out, he rose from the shadows and crept forward. He made it to the back door just in time to catch it before it closed. He and XO silently stalked the flat-booty Mexican until she made it back to her apartment. Just as she was closing the door, Murda stuck his steel-toe boot in the doorway.

173

"What the…" a shocked Auntie Dee called out at the intrusion.

She didn't get anything else out by the time Murda's body had knocked the door all the way open and snatched the little woman by the throat. She desperately tried to fight Murda off her, but it was no use. He was too strong. XO quickly searched the apartment, making sure no one else was there, while Murda beat and choked Auntie Dee.

"Bitch! You better shut the fuck up before I kill you." His words had the desired effect.

When Murda tore her clothes off of her, Auntie Dee knew what time it was. She started to fight back again, only to surmise that she was atoning for her past sins. Her past had somehow caught up with her, and even though she didn't know her two attackers, she knew without a shadow of a doubt that they were somehow tied to it all.

"Bitch, we about to send a message to them faggott ass little nephews of yours. Thanks to Alissa, we know everything that we need to know about all of you. If you shut the fuck up and take this dick, you'll live. If you scream out one time, I'm gone kill you. You got that?" Murda asked her as his hands fondled her now exposed breasts. "You got it, bitch!?"

She feebly nodded her head up and down while her body trembled with fear.

Murder didn't mind raping Auntie Dee. Her big ass tits had his dick rock hard. XO, on the other hand, didn't enjoy the act at all. However, they had all come to the agreement after Wes' death that they were sending the TIO clique a message like no other.

"Nothing and nobody was sage! Their women would be raped, children slaughtered until they all died one by one!"

With that being said, they brutally raped and beat Auntie Dee within inches of her life! Murda wanted to kill her, but C1ty felt the message would be stronger if she was left alive. So, they left her laying on the floor badly beaten and violated, desperately fighting to hold on to the little bit of life she had left inside of her.

Later on that night, MoMo would lose the last drop of decency he had left in him when he walked inside of the apartment and found his auntie naked and bleeding on the floor. He held her naked body in his arms and cried until the paramedics arrived.

*****

Spank-G sat in the big leather chair he had in his study. He'd just finished reading the newspaper. The recent string of homicides had him in a wonderous mood. His plan was going off without a hitch. Soon, this entire section of the city would be under siege. The old adage was true, "Revenge was a dish best served cold."

Just then, his cell phone buzzed on his desk. He took the blunt he was smoking out of his mouth before answering it. When he answered the phone, he held it to his ear and listened for a moment. When he spoke, it was only two words. Two simple words that would have a lasting effect.

"Do it."

The caller on the other end hung up the phone. Her orders were clear, and she would carry them out without question or delay. She removed the pillow from under Auntie Dee's head. The movement caused Auntie Dee to wake up. When she saw the white girl with the Harley Quinn hairdo standing over her, Auntie Dee was confused.

The evil smirk on the white girl's face and the pillow in her hands left little to the imagination. Auntie Dee knew she had been foolish to think she would escape death so easily and not atone for her sins. As the white girl placed the pillow over her and began suffocating her, Auntie Dee smiled softly to herself. *Finally, it is over*, was Auntie Dee's final thought.

Satisfied that her mission was complete, she removed the pillow, bent down, and kissed the now dead Auntie Dee on her lips. A sinister euphoria spread throughout the white girl's body. She slowly stood up and walked out of the hospital room.

Spank-G was leaving a message of his own, "No prisoners, only casualties!"

Chapter 27

MoMo sat on the middle of the worn-down couch in Auntie Dee's living room with a fifth of Hennessy dangling between his fingertips and a blunt of weed between his lips. He'd been up for three days without any sleep, running from demons that weren't going anywhere.

Before finding out about Auntie Dee, all MoMo had ever done was smoke weed and drink. Guilt was the reason the cocaine was on the coffee table in front of him. There were about four and half grams left of the initial ounce that he began with. Three empty Hennessey bottles lay in different places on the floor. Broken pieces of glass on the floor were the only evidence of the fourth empty bottle that was thrown against the wall during a violent outburst, when the wave of guilt first washed over his body.

"Damn, Auntie, I didn't know. I'm so sorry, Auntie. All this shit is my fucking fault! I swear to God, I didn't know. I thought doing a favor for the OG would be good for all of us. Plus, you always told us to chase the bag. Auntie, I was chasing my chicken!" He raised the bottle up to his lips. After two big swallows, MoMo let out a loud burp. "Fuuuuuuck!" he shouted loudly.

He quickly stood to his feet and began pacing the living room back and forth. The feel of his boots crunching the pieces of glass that he trampled over as he paced was inaudible, drowned out by the deep sounds of his ragged and raspy breathing. The sound was reminiscent of a wounded large animal on a long trek back to its den or layer.

"I fucked up. I know it. It's up to me to make this shit right! I—" His loud rant was interrupted by the sound of the loud banging coming from the front door.

MoMo looked at the door with an ugly mean mug on his face, angry that someone would interrupt him. He started to answer it but decided being in his own world was way more important. He continued to pace back and forth.

The loud banging sounded again, as whoever it was outside the apartment began pounding on the door again. The sound grew louder. This pissed MoMo off. He'd just turned and was pacing away from the door when the sound of the pounding started the second time. He was in mid-step, yet he spun around and closed the distance between him and the door in two large steps.

When he unlocked the door and snatched it open, he was ready to rip a new hole in the ass of whomever it was that was fucking with him. That was until he saw the face of his little cousin, T.G.

"Fuck you up in here shouting at? Nigga, you good?" T.G. didn't wait for MoMo to respond.

On full goon mode, he brushed past MoMo with his banger in his hand. Turned the fuck up and ready to go! T.G. thought the yelling he heard when he walked up to the apartment was due to MoMo getting into it with someone. Whatever problem MoMo was having, T.G. was ready to solve. Quickly, T.G. stormed through the apartment searching for a victim.

MoMo closed the front door without answering. While T.G. was storm trooping through the apartment, MoMo walked over to the couch, sat down, and snorted another couple of lines of the cocaine.

"Nigga, you in here yelling at yo'self?" T.G. asked MoMo when he came back into the living room. "Nigga, dat's coke?"

MoMo looked at T.G. with a weird, funny look on his face. In his mind, he was wondering if T.G. was fucking retarded for asking that stupid ass question. Of course, it was coke. What the fuck did it look like? He made two more lines and snorted them. He leaned his head back so the dope could drain from his nose down the back of his throat.

"MoMo! Muthafucka, you just gone sit yo' punk ass on that couch and ignore me like yo' ass can't hear me or something?" The sight of T.G. standing over him angrily glaring down on him would scare the shit out of most niggaz. MoMo wasn't most niggaz.

"First off, my nigga, you need to pipe down with all that yelling and shit. Nigga, we ain't in the muthafuck'n army. A nigga ain't ignoring you. I'm not in the mood to be answering no dumb ass questions. Nigga, dat's coke?" he mimicked T.G. "Yeah, it's coke, nigga! What the fuck it look like?"

"What the fuck, nigga! Mo, you throwing me off, brah. I know a nigga hurting right now. My nigga, we all hurting. I'm not 'bout to sit here and judge you, my nigga, so don't think that. But fucking with that shit to ease your pain and cope ain't the way to go." All the anger that was in him instantly dissolved.

MoMo tilted the bottle of Hennessey and took another swallow. The bottle was now a little less than halfway full.

"T, you gotta do you. If you don't like the way I'm dealing with my shit, don't let that bother you. Do you and I'mma do me, my nigga."

T.G. didn't want MoMo to think he was getting on him about the coke. He just wanted to let MoMo know that he was worried about him. The problem was, T.G. wasn't an emotional nigga. He was trying to show his love the best way he could. Realizing he was going about the shit the wrong way, he sat down on the couch next to MoMo and grabbed the bottle of Henn. T.G. was missing Auntie Dee too. She was more like a mom instead of an aunt. Auntie Dee was a major figure in their lives. It was going to be hard as fuck trying to embrace and deal with each day with her no longer being there.

He looked at MoMo, wrongfully believing that he could feel his pain. Thinking their pain was equal. His thoughts of empathy would fly out of the single apartment window if he had any clue that Auntie Dee's murder was behind MoMo's betrayal. That's why their hurt could never be the same. MoMo's pain was magnified by his guilt and shame.

"Niggaz is worried 'bout you, Mo. You ain't answered yo' phone in days. Nobody had a clue where you was at or nothing."

"If that's the case, fuck is you doing here?" The effects of the cocaine and alcohol were clearly visible. Sweat poured down MoMo's face like water.

For the first time, while sitting on the couch, T.G. began to pay attention to the state of the apartment. It wasn't completely fucked up, but there was shit all over the place. Trash and broken glass were scattered all over the floor. Dirty dishes, some with left-over food, were on the coffee table. T.G. looked to the side of the couch and saw an empty pizza box on the floor. There were two old, stale slices of pepperoni covered with ants still in the box. MoMo smelled like one of the homeless muthafuckas down in the Tenderloin District.

"Nigga, we gotta clean this muthafucka up, Mo. Dee would kick yo' muthafuck'n ass if she saw the way you had her shit looking right now."

MoMo looked around at the living room. He blinked his eyes like he was just now noticing the trash and junk for the first time. Then, as if T.G. told the world's funniest joke, MoMo burst into laughter. After a few seconds, T.G. joined in the laughter, and the both of them sat and laughed hysterically. They looked like two patients at a mental institution.

"I can hear her now. Muthafucka, I know you done lost your muthafuck'n last mind having my shit looking like a downtown alley," MoMo impersonated Auntie Dee. They laughed some more.

"I know yo' ass see the way I clean my shit and keep it on point, and you bring yo' little dirty ass in here! Trynna make my shit look like yo' house. Now, nephew, clean my muthafuck'n shit up! And let me get a few dollars so I can run to the store," T.G. mimicked their late auntie.

They continued their little tirade for a few minutes longer. Talking shit like they were Auntie Dee and laughing. Desperately trynna find a way to mask the hurt they both felt. After about four or five minutes, T.G. got up and started cleaning the apartment. MoMo moved the plate of coke so it wouldn't be disturbed, and joined in with the clean-up.

De'Kari

Chapter 28

The sounds of Boys II Men "The End of the Road" played through the speakers of the church. Asking no one in particular why the good times must always come to a heartbreaking end. As always, the song played on the memories of all in attention of today's funeral. Sending each person down their own personal trip through the weary streets of Memory Lane. Forcing each person to deal with the forgotten pain of their own lost loved ones. Brothers, sisters, cousins, mothers, fathers, and friends. Most of whom were tragically stolen way too early due to the senseless bloodshed attributed to street violence. Not a single face in attendance was dry.

Dell, the oldest of the four brothers, sat with his pain visibly on his face, in the front row of the church. The weight of his personal guilt caused his slender shoulders to sag on his 6'2" frame. Dell believed since he was the oldest brother, the first-born son, that it was his responsibility to make sure all of his younger brothers were okay, safe, and taken care of. He looked to his left at the brother closest to him in age, Don.

With his brown skin, curly tapered hair, and ducktail, Don looked like he should've been a Calvin Klein or Tommy Hilfiger model instead of the killer that he was. If anyone didn't know if gangstas cried, looking at these brothers still wouldn't answer the question. They, in fact, were not gangstas, but they were killers. And, yes, killers cried.

C1ty wasn't in the church with his two older brothers. He couldn't be. If Dell thought he felt guilty for Wes' death, he couldn't begin to imagine the hellish guilt trip that weighed heavily on the shoulders of his now youngest brother. No one could tell C1ty that Wes' death wasn't his fault. He was the unofficial leader of the family. He was the brains behind the formation of the 357 Mobb. He was also the one who decided that the Mobb go out to the auditorium that fateful day the funk started.

183

The Mobb had just hit for a big score with their latest bank heist. It was G-Baby's birthday, and C1ty thought it was a good idea for everybody to go out to relax while at the same time show their support and love to the newest up-and-coming star of the Bay Area's rap world, Skrew.

Never in a million years would C1ty have ever predicted that his decision that night would set off a string of events that would lead up to this dreadful day. He used the back of his left hand to wipe away the rogue tears that escaped his eyes, looking for freedom on his young, dark face.

C1ty couldn't afford to be caught all up in his feelings today, for the same reason he couldn't be inside of the church mourning the death of his baby brother. He had to be on point.

C1ty was a firm believer in karma. He wasn't about to let them TIO niggaz slide through and disrespect his brother's funeral like they had done Bubz's funeral. Bubz was the second ever TIO casualty, but the first casualty of this war. The day of Bubz's funeral, The Mobb shot up the entire funeral, killing Bubz's mother and a couple of other TIO members. C1ty wasn't about to allow them niggaz to do the same thing to his brother's funeral.

"Jeff, how that shit looking down yo' way?" C1ty spoke into the wireless comms concealed in his free hand.

"Shit, family, everything's everything down on my end. This rain fucking with a nigga's vision a little bit, but I already told my little ones we yanking on the first thing moving!" Jeff to Da Left responded. The words came through loud and clear in the hidden earpiece that C1ty was wearing.

Jeff to Da Left was the boss of the respected and feared Gas Nation out of West Oakland. He also was C1ty's older cousin. As a safety precaution for the funeral, C1ty reached out to his big cousin for support. He was serious about not letting muthafuckas disrespect his brother's funeral.

C1ty had become oblivious to the rain as he stood outside of the church. His mind was on the hell he was about to bring down on Lil' Dooka and his Blythedale clique. His attention was concentrated on making sure nobody fucked things up to-day for them.

"Alright, my nigga, keep me posted." If anybody did try something today, C1ty was ready to wake their muthafuck'n shit up.

Though he was doing his best to concentrate on watching the street, his mind flashed back to almost three years earlier, back to the night of Wes' high school senior prom.

It was a bittersweet night for Wes McDaniel. He was a seventeen-year-old senior graduating from Mission High School. This particular night was a night that all high school students looked forward to. It was Mission High School's Senior Prom. A night Wes had looked forward to all school year like the rest of his class. That was until he learned a month ago that prom night would fall on the four-year anniversary of the death of his parents.

It was a rainy April night in San Francisco. The McDaniels were out celebrating twenty-four years of marriage. That night, they were killed in a head-on collision with a drunk driver, while they were returning home from dinner.

Seventeen-year-old Wes was finding it hard to be excited about it being prom night. With constant memories of his parents and their love invading his mind, he felt ashamed that he would possibly consider enjoying a celebration on the very eve of the night they lost their lives. Wes thought that was self-ish.

He sat in his room in a pair of boxers and a tank top, star-ing at a photo of his parents. He'd finally made his mind up that he wouldn't attend the prom. Saddened about his deci-sion, he was willing to live with it because he felt it was the only possible choice for him to make.

It took a long discussion with C1ty that night to get Wes to snap out of his sullen mental state. In that discussion, C1ty had to get his little brother to realize that their parents wouldn't want any of them handicapping their own lives behind their parents' tragedy. Their parents lived a long, happy, loving life and would want their children to have the opportunity to experience the same for themselves.

Gradually, Wes came out of his saddened state. He went to his senior prom and had the time of his life. Loud, excited, and drunk out of his mind, Wes called C1ty at 2:45 in the morning. He was at the Embassy Suites with the school's two sexiest twins, Candy and Brandy. Candy was the captain of the cheerleading squad, and Brandy was the school's track and field sprint champion. Both were drop-dead gorgeous, and they were Wes' play toys for the night. Wes called C1ty to thank him for talking him into going to the prom, and to share the good news about the twins.

"C1ty, you're the best brother a nigga could ask for, my nigga. You're always looking out for me, and that's why you're my favorite brother. I know you'll never let anything happen to me! I love you, C1ty!" Wes declared in the phone before hanging up and enjoying the twins.

Those last words played over in C1ty's mind as his eyes betrayed him and released a fresh wave of tears down his face. A fresh wave of pain also washed over his body. He looked at the doors of Corner Stone Baptist Church, and for the hundredth time that day, he swore he would give anything in the world to bring his little brother back to life.

When the doors to the church opened, X.O. and Murda were the first ones out the doors. They both wore long, black, leather trench coats. The ones like they wore back east in the nineties. The brothers both carried AR-15s under the leather coats. They weren't taking any chances either. They both scanned the streets with their eyes like eagles searching an open field for prey.

The tension was high as the pallbearers followed the two brothers out of the church. This was the exact same moment weeks earlier that they had interrupted Bubz's funeral with a barrage of angry bullets that sliced through the day and bodies like razor blades sliced through cocaine white. Everyone was nervous but on point, anticipating a form of retaliation that would never come. At least not at that moment. Not that day!

De'Kari

Chapter 29

Gabby carried the plate of untouched food back into the kitchen, confused and worried. She'd gotten up early this morning after only getting a few hours of sleep to cook Lil' Dooka breakfast, hoping that it would make him feel better. He hadn't eaten anything since yesterday morning. He barely spoke to her at all. He just sat in the room drinking syrup and smoking blunt after blunt, with two Dracos on the floor on either side of his feet and one on the bed.

When she first heard the news about Aunt Dee, Gabby expected him to take it hard, just not as hard as this. Shit, he hadn't paid her any attention even though she walked around the house in next to nothing. She had on a powder-blue, sheer bra and boy shorts set. It was one of his favorites, yet he'd acted like he'd never even seen her as she walked around. All he did was smoke and drink and fuck with them damn guns.

Frustrated, Gabby slammed the plate of food down onto the counter with enough force to spill eggs and bacon on the counter and crack the plate. Two of the Hungry Jack biscuits rolled off the counter and hit the floor. She felt her emotions beginning to get the best of her. She placed her hands on the countertop and hung her head down low in preparation for the tears that she could feel welling up in her eyes.

"Fuck this shit!" Gabby fought back the tears and slammed her fist down on the counter next to the plate. She straightened her body and spun around. A spark of newfound determination ignited behind the orbs of her eyes. With this newfound determination, she took off in a march and stormed down the hallway, her thick thighs shaking as her legs crashed fiercely down with each step. No one could see her honey-golden ass cheeks bounce ferociously up and down with each step.

Lil' Dooka didn't even look up toward the sound of the loud bang the door made when Gabby came bursting into the room. He didn't see her big breasts jumping under the sheer material as she stomped across the room toward him.

"Now listen here, muthafucka! I know you're going through some shit right now, but you need to pull yo' mutha-fuck'n head out yo' black ass and get a grip. All you've done for days is sat there getting high with that sorry ass mutha-fuck'n, sad, pitiful look on ya pathetic ass face. You need to get the fuck up and go wash yo' stanking ass so you can get your shit together and be useful!" Gabby had never in her life spoken to Lil' Dooka in such a tone. She was beyond frustrated, and it showed.

Lil' Dooka slowly lifted his head and looked at Gabby. He didn't know if he was tripping or if she had really talked to him like that. The scowl on her face told him it wasn't his imagination. She had actually said that shit.

"Bitch, have you lost your muthafuck'n mind? Who the fuck do you think you're talking to, bitch!" Gabby saw a hint of that old fire burning deep behind his pupils. She wasn't about to back down.

"Bitch? Really, Deandre? So, I'm a bitch now?" She sounded like a wounded bird. Her voice was barely a whisper. Then the veil lifted, and she fed his ass both barrels. "No, muthafucka! You the bitch! Sitting in here moping and sniveling. Hiding from life and reality just like a little. Bitch. Ass. Nigga!" She let the last three words sound bitter, pronouncing each and every syllable like they were poisonous.

She didn't know he could move so fast. Like the rarest of black lightning, he shot up from the bed. His hand was around her throat before she ever realized he moved. He had a savage look in his eyes as he forced her to back pedal until she crashed into the wall next to the open door. On the other side of her was a long wooden dresser.

Gabby's huge breasts rose and fell as fear gripped her, causing her breathing to become heavy. She was happy that she'd managed to make him snap out of his funk. Yet, she was fearful of what he would do to her.

"You think I'm weak, bitch!" he growled. His face was only inches away from hers. "Is that it? Yo' stupid ass thought this shit put some fear in me. Made me soft!" His free hand shot up and smacked the shit out of her. "Hiding? That's what the fuck you thought I was doing? Hiding from reality?"

Gabby was too terrified to respond. He had never raised his hand to her, but secretly, she loved that thug shit.

"You think I'mma bitch, huh?" He snatched her from the wall and forced her over toward the dresser. He spun her around so that his chest pressed up against her back as he softly growled into her ear. "Naaw, bitch, I'mma show you who's the bitch!"

He pushed her head down, forcing her to bend over the dresser. The fear that Gabby was feeling earlier instantly left. She was glad to finally have her daddy back. Her pussy became wet instantly the moment he tore the sheer material of the boy shorts off of her. He pulled his dick out of the hole in his boxers and positioned it at the opening of her pussy. He bent down close to her ear and said, "Bitch, take dick like you about to." With one thrust, he shoved his dick deep into her wet, hot pussy.

The feel of his hard, throbbing dick pressing firmly into her combined with her love of that gangsta shit made her explode on contact. She was so excited that her pussy gushed from the powerful orgasm. Cum shot out of her like a land geyser. The sight of the milky white cream spraying out from around his big black dick made Lil' Dooka go ape shyt!

He pulled his eight-inch pole out of her pussy. Buckets of cum shot and spilled out of Gabby. She didn't have a clue what was going on. All she knew was she was in Heaven as he forced his way back into her and fucked her like he had a point to prove. The dresser made loud booming sounds as it banged repeatedly against the bedroom wall.

Over the course of time, locked away inside of the room, Lil' Dooka had been going through a transformation. It seemed muthafuckas weren't going to respect his mind until he first forced them to respect his gangsta, which was what the fuck he was about to do!

As he stared blankly at the sight of Gabby's phat ass violently shaking, aftershocks caused by his powerful thrusts, thoughts of murder and revenge were all that was on his mind. The thoughts drove him to grip Gabby's ass cheeks firmly and drive himself even deeper into the depths of her womb.

Manically, he fucked her. Repeatedly grunting and growling like a wild animal. The sounds and the good dick were driving Gabby mad with lust. She forced a hand between her breasts and the dresser and squeezed her nipple, tweaking it until another breathtaking orgasm stole the strength from her body.

Lil' Dooka felt her pussy muscles spasm. He grabbed a handful of her hair and really drove home. Pounding over and over, slamming his dick repeatedly, again and again, in and out of her hot, juicy pussy until he finally exploded, letting out a fierce roar as he did!

Chapter 30

T.G. was tired as fuck. He finally gave his weak knees a rest when he dropped down onto the couch. He wasn't the manual labor type of nigga. Cleaning Auntie Dee's apartment back up after the mess MoMo had created kicked his young ass. He would have loved an ice-cold Pepsi right then but was too tired to go to the store.

MoMo plopped down on the couch next to him, more exhausted than T.G. was. T.G. wouldn't let MoMo snort any more of the cocaine while they cleaned. He told MoMo that he needed to get some rest so he could get his mind right. Initially, MoMo protested. Finally, he gave in because he knew T.G. was right. MoMo couldn't remember the last time he ate. He knew the pizza was the last thing he had eaten, he just couldn't recall when that was.

"Nigga, you gone tell me now what all that yelling yo' ass was up in here doing was about?" T.G. asked MoMo.

They were first cousins. Not only that, but they had grown up from the dirt together. This made them closer than brothers. Although the shit that MoMo had to tell a nigga would no doubt break T.G.'s heart, MoMo knew the love that T.G. had for him wouldn't go anywhere. Still, he asked himself if he was sure he wanted to open his heart and spill his guts. The burden he carried was far too heavy. Perhaps sharing some of the burden with his cousin would be a good idea. At least the guilt of carrying the burden alone would be gone.

"My nigga, I don't think you wanna know what that was about." MoMo stalled, hoping T.G. would persist.

"Ain't nothing that bad, MoMo. Nigga, dis forever Greezy, and you know that. On the spirit of BR, my nigga, it ain't shit under the sun that you can't tell me." Whatever it was that was fucking with MoMo, T.G. didn't think it was really that serious.

Little did he know, MoMo's burden was heavy!

MoMo questioned himself again. Wondering if he should betray himself and his actions. Reluctantly, he finally decided to throw caution to the wind and say fuck it. He opened his mouth and released the truth of his betrayal from the confines of his soul.

While he listened, T.G.'s heart sank lower and lower. How could MoMo do some fuck nigga shit like he did? How could he betray the family's trust? Without realizing it, T.G. had wrapped his hand around his Glock 20. The 10mm magically slid off his hip. There was only one way to deal with a fuck nigga. One way to punish treason!

T.G.'s hand tightly squeezed the butt of the Glock 20. MoMo didn't see the lone tear as it slid down T.G.'s eye. T.G. didn't know if he could kill MoMo, but the laws of the underworld stated he had to. He cut his eyes cunningly at MoMo, who sat with his head bowed and eyes closed. He slowly raised the Glock up to MoMo's head.

Just before he pulled the trigger, an image of Baby Reno popped into his head. It was the first time they all had hung out on the hill since Lil' Dooka and them got shot at Jordan High School. Four people got shot that day. Lil' Dooka and Micah both took bullets in their ass. Edwin got hit in his arm, and little Shianne took two bullets. Her getting shot saved Nordy's life. She got shot in the leg and stomach. The bullet to her leg caused her to fall, tripping Nordy. Him stumbling over Shianne was the reason the two slugs traveling on a course intended for his head missed.

They all laughed about it on the Hill once Lil' Dooka was released from the hospital. BR was the main nigga getting on Lil' Dooka's case about getting shot in the ass.

"Nigga, now dese bitches gone be saying yo' ass got Bunz of Steele!" he teased Lil' Dooka.

The memory of BR cleared T.G.'s mind, which was clouded with raw emotions from all the losses they'd taken. When the suckas took BR, it was their first loss ever. Back then, sliding and busting drills was something they did for fun because the little niggaz were all bored. They weren't out in the field like that, though. When them suckaz took BR, the family came together as one. Fuck the turfs, cliques, and gangs. TIO was a family, and "Forever Greezy" was their motto. It was all for BR.

T.G. lowered his banger. By now, the tears ran the 100-meter dash down his face from both eyes. He wiped his face before MoMo could see the evidence of his pain. Then he told him, "Don't even sweat that shit. We gone fix this shit and push on like we always do, nigga. It's forever Greezy!"

MoMo opened his eyes and looked at his cousin. He had expected T.G. to go off on him. After all, T.G. was the real goon. When he looked in T.G.'s eyes, all MoMo saw was unconditional luv. He started to say something, but somebody started banging loud on the front door. MoMo got up to answer it. He figured it was the rest of his brothas, which was good, because he needed them all to know what he just told T.G. MoMo had to get it all off his chest, and there was no better time than the present.

When he reached the front door, he paused and called over his left shoulder, "Forever Greezy!"

He opened the door and all the color drained from his face. MoMo looked like he'd seen a ghost.

"Nigga, fuck TIO and fuck Tre-4!" It was none other than C1ty himself. He stood just about four feet back from the doorway with a sawed-off Mossberg Pump in his hands, in all black with his long black dreadlocks hanging wildly down his back and over his shoulders. He looked scarier than the Grim Reaper himself.

MoMo didn't get a chance to react. The blast of the shotgun once C1ty pulled the trigger caught him in his abdomen and chest. The force of the blast lifted MoMo off his feet and sent him flying five feet back into the apartment!

De'Kari
To Be Continued…
Straight Beast Mode 2: Forever Greezy!
Coming Soon

Lock Down Publications and Ca$h Presents assisted publishing packages.

BASIC PACKAGE $499
Editing
Cover Design
Formatting

UPGRADED PACKAGE $800
Typing
Editing
Cover Design
Formatting

ADVANCE PACKAGE $1,200
Typing
Editing
Cover Design
Formatting
Copyright registration
Proofreading
Upload book to Amazon

LDP SUPREME PACKAGE $1,500
Typing
Editing
Cover Design
Formatting
Copyright registration
Proofreading
Set up Amazon account
Upload book to Amazon
Advertise on LDP Amazon and Facebook page

De'Kari

***Other services available upon request. Additional charges may apply
Lock Down Publications
P.O. Box 944
Stockbridge, GA 30281-9998
Phone # 470 303-9761

Submission Guideline

Submit the first three chapters of your completed manuscript to ldpsubmissions@gmail.com, subject line: Your book's title. The manuscript must be in a .doc file and sent as an attachment. Document should be in Times New Roman, double spaced and in size 12 font. Also, provide your synopsis and full contact information. If sending multiple submissions, they must each be in a separate email.

Have a story but no way to send it electronically? You can still submit to LDP/Ca$h Presents. Send in the first three chapters, written or typed, of your completed manuscript to:

LDP: Submissions Dept
Po Box 944
Stockbridge, Ga 30281

DO NOT send original manuscript. Must be a duplicate.

Provide your synopsis and a cover letter containing your full contact information.

Thanks for considering LDP and Ca$h Presents.

<u>NEW RELEASES</u>

A DOPEBOY'S DREAM by ROMELL TUKES
MONEY MAFIA by JIBRIL WILLIAMS
QUEEN OF THE ZOO by BLACK MIGO
MOB TIES 4 by SAYNOMORE
THE BRICK MAN by KING RIO
KINGZ OF THE GAME by PLAYA RAY
VICIOUS LOYALTY by KINGPEN
STRAIGHT BEAST MODE by DEKARI

Straight Beast Mode

By **Trai'Quan**
THE STREETS MADE ME IV
By **Larry D. Wright**
IF YOU CROSS ME ONCE II
By **Anthony Fields**
THE STREETS WILL NEVER CLOSE II
By **K'ajji**
HARD AND RUTHLESS III
THE BILLIONAIRE BENTLEYS II
Von Diesel
KILLA KOUNTY II
By **Khufu**
MONEY GAME II
By **Smoove Dolla**
A GANGSTA'S KARMA II
By **FLAME**
JACK BOYZ VERSUS DOPE BOYZ
A DOPEBOY'S DREAM III
By **Romell Tukes**
MURDA WAS THE CASE II
Elijah R. Freeman
THE STREETS NEVER LET GO II
By **Robert Baptiste**
AN UNFORESEEN LOVE III
By **Meesha**
KING OF THE TRENCHES II
by **GHOST & TRANAY ADAMS**

MONEY MAFIA

De'Kari
By **Jibril Williams**

QUEEN OF THE ZOO II
By **Black Migo**

THE BRICK MAN II
By King Rio

VICIOUS LOYALTY II
By Kingpen

<u>**Available Now**</u>

RESTRAINING ORDER **I & II**
By **CA$H & Coffee**

LOVE KNOWS NO BOUNDARIES **I II & III**
By **Coffee**

RAISED AS A GOON I, II, III & IV

BRED BY THE SLUMS I, II, III

BLAST FOR ME I & II

ROTTEN TO THE CORE I II III

A BRONX TALE I, II, III

DUFFLE BAG CARTEL I II III IV V VI

HEARTLESS GOON I II III IV V

A SAVAGE DOPEBOY I II

DRUG LORDS I II III

CUTTHROAT MAFIA I II

KING OF THE TRENCHES
By **Ghost**

LAY IT DOWN **I & II**

LAST OF A DYING BREED I II

BLOOD STAINS OF A SHOTTA I & II III

By **Jamaica**

LOYAL TO THE GAME I II III

LIFE OF SIN I, II III

By **TJ & Jelissa**

BLOODY COMMAS I & II

SKI MASK CARTEL I II & III

KING OF NEW YORK I II,III IV V

RISE TO POWER I II III

COKE KINGS I II III IV

BORN HEARTLESS I II III IV

KING OF THE TRAP I II

By **T.J. Edwards**

IF LOVING HIM IS WRONG…I & II

LOVE ME EVEN WHEN IT HURTS I II III

By **Jelissa**

WHEN THE STREETS CLAP BACK I & II III

THE HEART OF A SAVAGE I II III

MONEY MAFIA

By **Jibril Williams**

A DISTINGUISHED THUG STOLE MY HEART I II & III

LOVE SHOULDN'T HURT I II III IV

RENEGADE BOYS I II III IV

PAID IN KARMA I II III

SAVAGE STORMS I II

AN UNFORESEEN LOVE I II

De'Kari

By **Meesha**

A GANGSTER'S CODE I &, II III

A GANGSTER'S SYN I II III

THE SAVAGE LIFE I II III

CHAINED TO THE STREETS I II III

BLOOD ON THE MONEY I II III

By **J-Blunt**

PUSH IT TO THE LIMIT

By **Bre' Hayes**

BLOOD OF A BOSS **I, II, III, IV, V**

SHADOWS OF THE GAME

TRAP BASTARD

By **Askari**

THE STREETS BLEED MURDER **I, II & III**

THE HEART OF A GANGSTA I II& III

By **Jerry Jackson**

CUM FOR ME I II III IV V VI VII

An **LDP Erotica Collaboration**

BRIDE OF A HUSTLA **I II & II**

THE FETTI GIRLS **I, II& III**

CORRUPTED BY A GANGSTA I, II III, IV

BLINDED BY HIS LOVE

THE PRICE YOU PAY FOR LOVE I, II ,III

DOPE GIRL MAGIC I II III

By **Destiny Skai**

WHEN A GOOD GIRL GOES BAD

By **Adrienne**

THE COST OF LOYALTY I II III

By **Kweli**

206

A GANGSTER'S REVENGE **I II III & IV**

THE BOSS MAN'S DAUGHTERS I II III IV V

A SAVAGE LOVE **I & II**

BAE BELONGS TO ME I II

A HUSTLER'S DECEIT I, II, III

WHAT BAD BITCHES DO I, II, III

SOUL OF A MONSTER I II III

KILL ZONE

A DOPE BOY'S QUEEN I II III

By **Aryanna**

A KINGPIN'S AMBITON

A KINGPIN'S AMBITION **II**

I MURDER FOR THE DOUGH

By **Ambitious**

TRUE SAVAGE I II III IV V VI VII

DOPE BOY MAGIC I, II, III

MIDNIGHT CARTEL I II III

CITY OF KINGZ I II

NIGHTMARE ON SILENT AVE

By **Chris Green**

A DOPEBOY'S PRAYER

By **Eddie "Wolf" Lee**

THE KING CARTEL **I, II & III**

By **Frank Gresham**

THESE NIGGAS AIN'T LOYAL **I, II & III**

By **Nikki Tee**

GANGSTA SHYT **I II &III**

By **CATO**

De'Kari

THE ULTIMATE BETRAYAL

By **Phoenix**

BOSS'N UP **I , II & III**

By **Royal Nicole**

I LOVE YOU TO DEATH

By **Destiny J**

I RIDE FOR MY HITTA

I STILL RIDE FOR MY HITTA

By **Misty Holt**

LOVE & CHASIN' PAPER

By **Qay Crockett**

TO DIE IN VAIN

SINS OF A HUSTLA

By **ASAD**

BROOKLYN HUSTLAZ

By **Boogsy Morina**

BROOKLYN ON LOCK I & II

By **Sonovia**

GANGSTA CITY

By **Teddy Duke**

A DRUG KING AND HIS DIAMOND I & II III

A DOPEMAN'S RICHES

HER MAN, MINE'S TOO I, II

CASH MONEY HO'S

THE WIFEY I USED TO BE I II

By Nicole Goosby

TRAPHOUSE KING **I II & III**

KINGPIN KILLAZ I II III

STREET KINGS I II

PAID IN BLOOD **I II**

CARTEL KILLAZ I II III

DOPE GODS I II

By **Hood Rich**

LIPSTICK KILLAH **I, II, III**

CRIME OF PASSION I II & III

FRIEND OR FOE I II III

By **Mimi**

STEADY MOBBN' **I, II, III**

THE STREETS STAINED MY SOUL I II

By **Marcellus Allen**

WHO SHOT YA **I, II, III**

SON OF A DOPE FIEND I II

HEAVEN GOT A GHETTO

Renta

GORILLAZ IN THE BAY **I II III IV**

TEARS OF A GANGSTA I II

3X KRAZY I II

STRAIGHT BEAST MODE

DE'KARI

TRIGGADALE I II III

MURDAROBER WAS THE CASE

Elijah R. Freeman

GOD BLESS THE TRAPPERS I, II, III

THESE SCANDALOUS STREETS I, II, III

FEAR MY GANGSTA I, II, III IV, V

THESE STREETS DON'T LOVE NOBODY I, II

BURY ME A G I, II, III, IV, V

De'Kari
A GANGSTA'S EMPIRE I, II, III, IV

THE DOPEMAN'S BODYGAURD I II

THE REALEST KILLAZ I II III

THE LAST OF THE OGS I II III

Tranay Adams

THE STREETS ARE CALLING

Duquie Wilson

MARRIED TO A BOSS I II III

By Destiny Skai & Chris Green

KINGZ OF THE GAME I II III IV V VI

Playa Ray

SLAUGHTER GANG I II III

RUTHLESS HEART I II III

By Willie Slaughter

FUK SHYT

By Blakk Diamond

DON'T F#CK WITH MY HEART I II

By Linnea

ADDICTED TO THE DRAMA I II III

IN THE ARM OF HIS BOSS II

By Jamila

YAYO I II III IV

A SHOOTER'S AMBITION I II

BRED IN THE GAME

By S. Allen

TRAP GOD I II III

RICH $AVAGE

By Troublesome

FOREVER GANGSTA

GLOCKS ON SATIN SHEETS I II

By Adrian Dulan

TOE TAGZ I II III

LEVELS TO THIS SHYT I II

By Ah'Million

KINGPIN DREAMS I II III

By Paper Boi Rari

CONFESSIONS OF A GANGSTA I II III IV

By Nicholas Lock

I'M NOTHING WITHOUT HIS LOVE

SINS OF A THUG

TO THE THUG I LOVED BEFORE

By Monet Dragun

CAUGHT UP IN THE LIFE I II III

THE STREETS NEVER LET GO

By Robert Baptiste

NEW TO THE GAME I II III

MONEY, MURDER & MEMORIES I II III

By **Malik D. Rice**

LIFE OF A SAVAGE I II III

A GANGSTA'S QUR'AN I II III

MURDA SEASON I II III

GANGLAND CARTEL I II III

CHI'RAQ GANGSTAS I II III

KILLERS ON ELM STREET I II III

JACK BOYZ N DA BRONX I II III

A DOPEBOY'S DREAM I II

By Romell Tukes

De'Kari
LOYALTY AIN'T PROMISED I II

By Keith Williams

QUIET MONEY I II III

THUG LIFE I II III

EXTENDED CLIP I II

By **Trai'Quan**

THE STREETS MADE ME I II III

By **Larry D. Wright**

THE ULTIMATE SACRIFICE I, II, III, IV, V, VI

KHADIFI

IF YOU CROSS ME ONCE

ANGEL I II

IN THE BLINK OF AN EYE

By **Anthony Fields**

THE LIFE OF A HOOD STAR

By Ca$h & Rashia Wilson

THE STREETS WILL NEVER CLOSE

By K'ajji

CREAM I II

By Yolanda Moore

NIGHTMARES OF A HUSTLA I II III

By King Dream

CONCRETE KILLA I II

VICIOUS LOYALTY

By Kingpen

HARD AND RUTHLESS I II

MOB TOWN 251

THE BILLIONAIRE BENTLEYS

By Von Diesel

GHOST MOB

Stilloan Robinson

MOB TIES I II III IV

By SayNoMore

BODYMORE MURDERLAND I II III

By Delmont Player

FOR THE LOVE OF A BOSS

By C. D. Blue

MOBBED UP I II III IV

THE BRICK MAN

By King Rio

KILLA KOUNTY

By Khufu

MONEY GAME

By Smoove Dolla

A GANGSTA'S KARMA

By FLAME

KING OF THE TRENCHES II

by **GHOST & TRANAY ADAMS**

QUEEN OF THE ZOO

By **Black Migo**

BOOKS BY LDP'S CEO, CA$H

TRUST IN NO MAN

TRUST IN NO MAN 2

TRUST IN NO MAN 3

BONDED BY BLOOD

SHORTY GOT A THUG

THUGS CRY

THUGS CRY 2

THUGS CRY 3

TRUST NO BITCH

TRUST NO BITCH 2

TRUST NO BITCH 3

TIL MY CASKET DROPS

RESTRAINING ORDER

RESTRAINING ORDER 2

IN LOVE WITH A CONVICT

LIFE OF A HOOD STAR

Straight Beast Mode

CPSIA information can be obtained
at www.ICGtesting.com
Printed in the USA
LVHW021933240222
711933LV00010B/1034